THROUGH
A GLASS
DARKLY

Nancy L. Nix

authorHOUSE®

AuthorHouse™ LLC
1663 Liberty Drive
Bloomington, IN 47403
www.authorhouse.com
Phone: 1-800-839-8640

Published by AuthorHouse 09/23/2014

ISBN: 978-1-4969-4095-7 (sc)
ISBN: 978-1-4969-4096-4 (e)

It was a bitterly cold day for April, although the sun shone brightly. Anne held her coffee cup tightly as she watched the birds dance on her windowsill, eating the seed that had fallen from the feeder. The funeral was over, everyone had just left and this was the first time she had been alone all day. Thoughts of Luke sped through her mind, tripping one over the other, tumbling down and causing moisture to form behind her eyelids, a throbbing ache in her chest, making it difficult to swallow. Almost 65 years with this loving, wonderful giant of a man. Now, she was alone, no hand reaching out to her, no knowing smile or conspiratoral wink, no intimate jokes. The actualality of it all was almost too much to bear. So suddenly he was gone. One minute, he looked at her, smiled and kissed her goodnight and went to sleep, a sleep from which he never awoke. Finding him 5 days ago, that horrible morning, realizing she had been talking to the wall, that Luke had already gone. She knew where he was; that much was a comfort. Yes, she knew his staunch faith in God, how he put his trust in Jesus, how he lived his life. "Thank you, Lord, for that", she whispered, finally succumbing to the tears she had held back for the last 5 days. "Oh, Lord", she pleaded, for that was all she could manage. She knew this was the place she would find her peace, her solace, but still she wept. "Who could think an old heart like mine could love like it was still young?", she thought. All those years ago, Luke had smiled at her and John in the park. Her hand flew to her mouth, her tears stopping suddenly on a hiccup. John!! He didn't know and she had to tell him. He was 68 years old and it was probably about time. All those years with Luke. What a good, kind husband, what a great father he had been. Jolene and Bill had come along and they had been such a happy family. A good life, different from the life that she had been leading. John. She had to call him and have him come over. She had to talk with him and explain it all to him. Reaching for the phone, she dialed her eldest son's cell phone number.

John was back at his parents' home for the second time that day. Mom had wanted to have some time to herself, but within an hour, she had called and asked him to come over. "Don't tell your brother or sister, she had said, you come alone." John had lost his wife when the kids were just 3 and 4 years old, succumbing to breast cancer before they even knew there was a problem. He had never remarried and stayed very close to his folks, staying involved in their day to day lives. Dad's death had hit him hard, taking away his best friend for the second time. Mom had sounded a little strange over the phone and a little stressed and he hoped she was going to be able to cope with Dad's death all right. Mom and Dad had quite a love story, meeting in the park and falling instantly in love. John always thought that if Cathy had lived, their love would have been just as enduring and special. She had been gone almost 40 years now and he had never even come close to finding someone like her. He had dated over the years and had women friends with whom he went to dinner and plays and such, but none were serious or intimate and probably would never be. He rang the bell and in less than a minute, his mother stood before him.

"Honey, you could have just walked in," she said, leading the way to the kitchen. "I know, I didn't want to startle you or interrupt you," he said discreetly. She eyed him wryly and answered, "Don't worry, I had my cry already." She went to the coffee pot and poured them both a cup. Sitting down with her at the table, John went through the ritual of adding one sugar and a dab of cream to his coffee, waiting for his mother to broach whatever subject she had called him over to hear. She had merely said to him on the phone, "There is something quite urgent I need to speak with you about right away. Can you come over?" At first he thought it was some financial problem she needed help with, but the more he thought about it, the more it had sounded personal.

"John, there is something I have to tell you. Maybe I should have told you years ago, but there never seemed to be a need. And you and Dad were always so close." Closing her eyes, she ran her hand across her forehead. "What is it, Mom? Was Dad a bank robber or something?" He chuckled but his mother's expression remained grim. "What is it, Mom?, he said softly. It couldn't be that bad." His mother looked into his eyes and sighed. "There is no easy way to say it. I was married before I married Dad and he was missing in action, presumed dead. We were only married for six weeks and I didn't realize I was pregnant with you until right after I learned he was missing." Anne paused for breath and studied her son's stunned expression. "John, I know this is a lot to take in, but with Dad's passing, I thought you should know." He stared at her for a few seconds and then something akin to anger crossed his brow. "You think, Mom? I am almost 70 years old and you thought now would be a good time to tell me that the man I idolized all my life is not really my father?" John shook his head, pacing back and forth. Anne said nothing. "I need to get out for a while. Think," he said tersely, grabbing his coat. Anne sat alone in the house watching the clock as it ticked away. Should she have just gone to her grave and never told him? But it seemed so wrong to do that. He had a right to know who he really was. Finally, John came back, walked into the kichen, sat down and sighed, his anger disapated. "I guess I do understand why you did it that way, but I wished I had known a few years earlier. I would like to know about my father. Did you learn any details about his MIA status?" Anne thought back to the day she had met her beloved Jack. Carefree with an easy smile, curly brown hair and that wonderful laugh. John had looked so much like him at that age, it had taken her breath away. She was 17 and he was 21, their whole lives ahead of them.

Looking at the dance floor at all the young soldiers and sailors and marines, Anne gave a sigh. Almost all the boys in her senior class had enlisted in one of the services, many in the Navy because of Pearl Harbor. She watched as the couples glided by her on the floor. Suddenly, she felt an arm around her waist as she was swept onto the dance floor. Shocked, she glanced to where Mrs. Sheridan was chaperoning, but she was looking the other way. Angrily, she turned toward her unwelcomed partner and spat, "I don't like fresh....", but stopped in midsentence at laughing brown eyes and a sweet, smiling mouth, set in a strong jaw. "You don't like fresh what? Fruit, fresh milk, fresh air?" Her anger disappeared and although she knew she should be offended, she just couldn't be. She laughed and quipped, "I was going to say fresh men, but I can see that you are still a boy." His eyebrows shot up in amusement and he answered, "Just for that, I will have to marry you and show you the difference between a man and a boy." She blushed down to her toes at his forwardness, but she could not find the will to leave his arms. They danced and danced, ignoring the rest of the servicemen, much to Mrs. Sheridan's disapproval. That was a definite rule breaker, but Anne didn't care. Nothing mattered but Jack. She learned he was an Army Air pilot and he loved flying. The end of the evening came much too soon and Jack walked her the three blocks to her house. "May I see you tomorrow?" he asked. Anne saw the boy in him then, the way he anxiously awaited her answer, his uncertainty that it would be yes. But she did not want to tease and play games. She sensed there was something more with Jack, something urgent and rare and she nodded in acquiesance. They had seen each other every tomorrow for the next week. Then at the end of that unbelievable week, they were sititng on a blanket in the park of her small town eating lunch and Jack took her hand. Softly he said, "I ship out in 8 days. Anne, I love you and I want you to marry me. Please, let's get married tomorrow so we can be together before I leave." Anne knew what he meant, but she wanted the same. She gazed into his beautiful eyes, now pooled with longing and love. "My parents will never agree," she whispered. "Let's try," he had replied and they did. Anne's parents were not amiss to a long distance engagement, but they put their foot down at marriage. Then Anne suddenly remembered her mother was only 17 years older than she and her parents admitted (with help from her Grandma, Dad's mom) that she was married at 16 years old and Dad had only been 18 in WW I. Mom understood how it hurt to be separated from the man you loved and finally even Dad was convinced to let them marry if Anne lived with them while Jack was overseas. That was not a problem for any of them and plans were hastily made. Jack and Anne had forgotten about the 3 day wait for a blood test, so 4 days later, they were married in Anne's parents' parlor with her parents, her 2 sisters and brother and Grandma in attendance. It was the happiest day of Anne's life. Grandma graciously moved in to Anne's room for the duration of Jack's leave and gave them her little house on the property for privacy. For the next 4 days, nobody saw the newlyweds leave their little honeymoon cottage. Jack asked her if she still thought he was a boy and she was so filled with love, she threw her arms around him and burst into tears. This startled him and he started to apologize if he hurt her, but she shushed him and snuggled up to him. "You are definitely no boy," she smiled. He chuckled and held her even tighter. Anne couldn't remember if they ate, so great was their absorption in each other. When the day came for Jack to ship out, she thought her heart would break. Standing at the train station with many other servicemen, they held tight to each other's hands. Anne's parents and Grandma and the whole family were there. Jack had confided to Anne that he had no family and had been raised in an orphanage "that wasn't so bad". He loved the thought of belonging to Anne's family and starting one of his own. He was touched that everyone had showed up to see him off. "I will not cry and make this harder for you," Anne promised, heeding her Dad's advice. "But I will write every day and I will miss you every day and I will mark on the calandar the days until you come back to me." He kissed her gently. "I am not a religious man, but there must be a God because only God could make a girl like you." She thought she saw the hint of tears in his eyes as the whistle blew and the engineer cried, "Allll Aboard!" He quickly shook her father's hand, kissed her mother and sisters on the cheek (much to her 15 year old sister's delight!) and gravely shook her 10 year old brother's hand. "Look out for my wife, will ya?" he asked him. Her brother straightened up proudly proclaiming, "Nothing will happen to Anne on my watch, you can count on that brother!" Billy had been thrilled to acquire a brother and made no bones about it. Finally, he turned and took her in his arms. "My darling, darling Anne, I never knew I could love anyone so much. I just want this war over so I can be with you. I will come back, I promise." She clung to him the unshed tears choking in her throat, trying to keep her promise not to cry. "I'll be here," she whispered, "I promise." And one teardrop sealed their promise to each other, neither knowing whose tear it was. Then he was torn away, waving at her from the step of the train, smiling his beautiful smile. She waved until he was out of sight and then blindly turned and fell into her mother's comforting arms. She wrote diligently to him every day, but did not hear anything until 6 weeks after he had shipped out. Then as she was in her room writing yet another letter to Jack, the doorbell rang. Suddenly, her father was at her bedroom door with a gentle expression on his face. "Honey," he started, but she knew what had happened and she didn't want to know. Not Jack, not laughing, happy wonderful Jack. He was supposed to come home and start a family and have the family that he never had. "Daddy, don't say it, don't," she begged and flung herself into his arms. But they wanted to give the widow the telegram so she forced herself to go downstairs and thank them for coming in person to tell her.

"Please, she heard herself saying, "have some coffee. I won't be but a minute. This must have been very hard on you." She saw the surprised look on their faces, heard their polite refusal and watched them leave. The next three days were a blur. Her parents and siblings tiptoed around her as she sat in numbed silence. She started feeling nauseated and tired and didn't eat enough to keep a bird alive. She just couldn't keep anything down. She didn't tell anyone how she felt until one morning her mother caught her with her head in the toilet, vomiting and crying at the same time. Her heart was so broken she didn't want to live. Her mother gently cleaned her up and told her the glorious news that saved her life. Mom thought she might be pregnant with Jack's child! She could hardly believe it and cried happy tears this time. A trip to the family doctor proved what she already knew was true and the whole family reveled in the joy of her pregnancy. The telegram had said missing in action, presumed dead. There was still hope. And hope she did, for three long years. She had a beautiful son whom she named John (Jack's real name) and he was the darling of the family. Her brother had taken Jack's death very hard and the baby helped to soothe that a bit. He played with him a lot and offered to babysit. Her sisters were sympathetic, but they had gone on with their lives, as had everyone else in town. Then one day she got a letter in the mail. It was from Jack! Excitedly, she tore it open with joy. He was alive, she had a letter! But as she scanned it quickly, she realized it was a letter from three years ago, one that had gotten caught up in the mail. It was dated just one week before the knock at her door that had shattered her life. "My Darling Anne, it read, "Can you believe that we have been apart for almost six weeks? It seems like six years to me, I miss you so. I have received 3 of your letters and I know you wrote more. They will catch up with me, I am sure, one of these days! I only have a few minutes, because we are prepping for a mission (can't tell you anything) but I am glad to be flying that's for sure. Feel alive up there! Please give my regards to your family, especially my "brother" Billy! What a sweet kid. If I could have chosen a brother, he would have been just like him! Kiss the girls (but don't make them cry like Georgie Porgie, boy I must be tired) and hug your parents and Grandma. I can never begin to tell them how much it meant to me to be taken into the family like that. Can't wait until we can all be together around the Thanksgiving table and Christmas tree, things I have only dreamed about all my life. And for you, my most precious loved wife, there are not enough hugs and kisses in the world to show you how much I love you. Dream of me, my darling, for you are all I dream of. Your loving husband Jack". She knew then that he was not coming back. A three year old letter, his last one to her. She put away her hopes and dreams of seeing him again and concentrated on raising John. It was one day at the park, about 3 months later, that she was pushing John on the swings when she noticed a gentleman in an army uniform watching her. She glanced his way and then put her attention back on John. "Look Mommy, I go high", he chortled in his baby talk. Her heart squeezed. How she loved this child, this extension of Jack! She imagined this was how Jack was as a child. "Anne, is that you?" She looked up, startled and realized the serviceman was talking to her. Then she realized who it was. "Luke, Luke Crawford, oh it's good to see you!" She took his hand and shook it and smiled up at him. And it was good to see him. Luke had been her cousin's best friend for years and she knew him well. "Are you back for good?", she asked. That had been the question everyone was asking these days. "I am. I feel like I should go back, but my limp is keeping me stateside." She involuntarily looked down at his leg. "What happened?" He smiled wryly. "Well, it is called the million dollar wound, so I am going to be discharged, but I think I would rather take my chances over there than carry this around forever." She looked at him and said earnestly, "No, Luke, I would never wish for anyone to go back. I would rather you have the wound." Luke looked sheepishly at her. "I heard your husband went down in a plane. I am sorry." And then, to change the subject, he asked, "Is this your little boy?" Anne turned to John, who was still swinging and smiling but beginning to slow down. "Higher Mommy!" her chirped. Luke stepped up to the swing. "Here, allow me," he said and gave the swing a hefty push. Anne was alarmed, but heard John squeal and Luke laugh and the sound of them together was like a balm to her soul. That was the start and they married after a year. John, being so young, just forgot that Luke was not his father and nobody in the family ever dissuaded him of the idea. And Luke was an ideal father.

"And that is it. That's all I can tell you. I only knew him for a couple of weeks. We were so young, but I think if he had come back, we would have been happy together. As it was, John, all things work together for the good of those who love the Lord. I don't know why it worked out this way, but didn't we have a good life with our family?" Mom looked at him, her eyes pleading for him to answer in the affirmative, but that was no hardship. His life had been wonderful with his family and his Dad, well Luke was his Dad after all, was someone after whom he had fashioned his own life. He smiled and took his mother's hand. "Dad was a perfect family man, I love my brother and sister and I had a great life and an even greater mom." She smiled tentatively at him then and patted the hand that held her's. "Thanks, Sweetie. Well, I am glad I told you. I feel better now. I was always afraid that someone would spill the beans and then you would feel different and I didn't want that for you." John stood up from the table. "Where did he disappear, did they say?" Anne took the cups and put them in the sink. "Yes, in France. After the war, some of his buddies and even some government personnel went searching, but they didn't come up with anything. The locals couldn't tell them anything. There was so much confusion and trauma over there at that time. It's funny your father should have crashed in France, because he was French, at least that is what the orphanage told him of his parentage. It's fitting he should be buried in his parents' homeland." John paced the kitchen. Something was eating at him, something he wanted to do. "His buddies, are any of them still alive?" he asked his mother. "Oh, I don't know, honey. I didn't really know them. They just sent me a letter telling me what they did and by that time, Dad and I were married. Dad offered to go over and see what he could find, but John, that was so awkward. I mean if the Army and his buddies couldn't find anything, what could Dad find?" She shook her head, as if it was a bad dream, and walked toward the coffeepot. "More coffee?" she asked. "What, uh no thanks, Mom. I should get going or do you want me to stay?" She looked a little shaken. "That would be nice, if you don't mind," she allowed. John had no one to go home to. His kids were grown and gone and Cathy gone all these years. "Goodnight, Mom, I am beat. I am going to bed and I suggest you do the same." He kissed her goodnight and headed for the guest room, the room that had been his many years before. "Goodnight, dear and thanks for staying," she smiled at him. He turned and looked at his beloved mother and watched as she walked toward the bedroom that she had shared with her husband for almost 69 years, or was it really only 66 years. All these years they had added three years onto their wedding day so we kids wouldn't suspect. A wave of grief hit him. "So long, Dad," he whispered. "No matter what, you were the greatest Dad in the world. Thanks for loving me."

John woke in the morning and had to think for a moment where he was. Ah, yes, his old room, the one that Dad and Mom had built on for him, when he turned 13, so he could have a room of his own. His little brother was only 4 and Dad said "an older guy needs his own space". Again, the grief hit him. Was it just a week ago that he had been at his parents' house for dinner and his Dad in great form, laughing and joking? He could not stop thinking of Luke as his Dad.

This was the wonderful man who had raised him, who had given him his time and wisdom and love. He was the loving grandfather of his children, the great grandfather of his grandchildren. He was his best friend. He adored this man and would honor his memory forever. But before him had been another man, a man who had not had a chance to be a father, who maybe would have loved him as much, possibly more (I don't know if that is possible) and had a different slant on his life, good or bad. Oh, it took nothing from Luke to want to know more of his biological father who, after all did not desert him but died fighting for his country. Would Mom understand? Well, damn it, he was 68 years old and he had to do what he knew he had to do. Mom, after all, was a woman and men and women had different ideas. He would talk with her over breakfast, because he knew through experience, there would definitely be breakfast!

He was not disappointed. Mom had a full spread. There were pancakes, bacon, eggs, coffee, juice ready for him. Sometimes he wondered if his mother ever slept. As they sat eating, he ventured onto the subject he had thought about in a dream, maybe a vision. It seemed like the thing he should do. "Mom, I really want to know more about my biological father. I mean, I loved Dad with all my heart, what a great guy to take me on and love me the way he did. I couldn't have asked for a better Dad, but I want to know about the guy that didn't get a chance to be my father. I want to find out about him." Mom looked a little stunned. "Well, honey, I think I told you everything I know. As I said, we only knew each other for a couple of weeks. I mean, I think he would have been a really good father to you, but I just can't tell you anymore." John dipped his head and concentrated on his pancakes. He was such a coward. Okay, he would just tell her. "Mom, I am going to France and see what I can find. I am going to ask questions within a 25 mile radius of where my father's plane went down and I am going to find out what happened to him. I mean, no one ever gave you an answer. No one ever said, 'well, we found a body and buried it'. I am not satisfied. I want to know what happened to him." John sipped his coffee and glanced over this cup to gauge his mother's reaction. She was dumbfounded. "Honey, no one knows what happened. I don't like to dwell on it, but I think he burned up in the crash. What else could have happened?" John put down his coffee cup. He chose his words carefully. "I don't know, Mama, but I have to find out." Anne's head jerked up. He had not called her Mama in years. He was really serious about this. She thought, at 68 years old, this would not hit him so hard, but she was wrong. How would she feel if she found out her beloved father was not really her Dad? She took a deep breath and said, ". Alright, I am going with you." If John could have been more shocked, he would not know how. His mother was 86 years old and could not make a trip abroad. "Mom, no you are in no shape to take a trip to France. I can take Bill or Luke", he protested, referring to his brother and son. But she would not be deterred. "He was, at one time, my most beloved husband and I cannot sit here while you go over there and try to find out about your parentage by yourself." The she stopped and gently touched his face. "John, dear, I loved your father will all my heart and I grieved so for him. If I could get some closure as to what happened to him, it would help me too." Tears ran down John's face and he was not a man given to his emotions. After Cathy had died, he thought he had locked them up tight. "Mama", he started, but could not finish. He held her hand that held his face and they both had an emotional moment, for lack of a better word. John was the first to collect himself. "Mama, after Dad, you are my best friend and since Dad is dead, I guess that puts you in first place." He knew he did not offend her, because she smiled that smile she smiled when she was so happy. She had loved Luke with all her heart and to know her firstborn loved him like that made her happy. "But you are elderly, Mom, I hate to say it, but you are. Hell, even I am considered elderly. I worry about you making a trip like that. I would never forgive myself if anything happened to you." Anne looked at him with pride and deep love. "My darling boy, could you forgive yourself for denying me of knowing what happened to your father and my very first love? You do not know what we had between us, the plans, the hopes, the dreams. Please, let me go with you. If I die on the trip home (which I will try not to do) I feel I would have done what I needed to do." She smiled up at him, the benign, motherly smile that unhinged him and persuaded him to give her whatever she wanted. He could see how his Dad and his biological father could be persuaded by a younger and beautiful Anne, but as far as he was concerned, she was still beautiful. He realized he did not know something very important. "Mom, what was my father's name?" Anne smiled and her eyes looked like she was seeing something far away. "Jack. Jack LaFontaine. For a short while I was Anne LaFontaine. And you were John LaFontaine". John thought about that for a moment. He had been John Crawford for as long as he could remember. It was a good name, a strong name. No, he couldn't give it up; that is who he was, but he thought for a moment about who John LaFontaine might have been.

May 25, 1944 Jack

Being 21 and newly married, having spent only 4 days and 5 nights with his lovely bride, there wasn't much that could take Jack's mind off marital bliss except for one thing-----flying. He had only been up a few times since he had been sent to England but he had heard the guys talk of a mission over Germany to do to them what they did to England, a reverse Blitzkrieg of sorts. Jack was itching to get back into the air. The only time he had flown were quick supply runs into London to help out the civilians. He hardly got his plane into the air and it was time to land again. He wanted a lengthy mission, one that kept him in the air, one that smacked those Germans down to their knees. Jack knew a lot of guys in his unit weren't too fond of Jews, so he hadn't said anything, but he wanted to strike one for the Jews. He knew a lot of people didn't believe it, but he had heard that there were death camps for Jews and other "undesirables". Some kids had called him a Jew when he was young and the way they had said it wasn't friendly. He had asked one of the nuns at the orphanage, Sister Mary John, in fact, the one nun who wrote him faithfully ever since he had been in the service, and she had told him he was not a Jew and not to worry about it. But when he had confided in the old Negro handyman, Davey who was a friend and confidant to all the boys in the orphanage, he had smiled and told him that "Jews were God's chosen people" and because of that they had always been persecuted. "The Jews didn't believe Jesus was the Messiah, the Saviour you see, so a lot of people don't like the Jews. Say Jews killed Jesus, but don't you believe it. People's always tryin' to pass the buck. We ALL killed Jesus, but He never stopped lovin' us. And God CHOSE the Jews to be His people, so I gotta say to be a Jew is somethin' special." He looked at Jack for a minute and said, "Yeah, you could be a Jew, but then I could be a black man." And he laughed that big hearty laugh of his that told Jack he could care less if he was purple with pink polka dots and then started back trimming the hedges. He would have asked him more, but the dinner bell had rung and he had run off to eat. He never had the opportunity to speak alone with Davey again for he died in his sleep the following night. The nuns broke the news with great gentleness, for they knew the place he held in the boys' hearts and a mass was said for Davey's soul. Jack thought that Davey's soul was in pretty good shape and he lost interest in God and Jesus after that, because the nuns never could quite make it real the way Davey did. "The old man wants to see you," Phelps told him, bringing him out of his reverie. He jumped up, making a quick inspection of himself before presenting himself to his C.O. The colonel was a pretty good sort, a little rigid, but Jack supposed he had to be in these circumstances. The colonel was a few years older than Jack, maybe 4 or 5 years, not long out of college and some flying time for sure. You could tell when someone had experience because they actually knew what they were talking about. Jack was admitted to the office and stood at attention until the colonel acknowledged him. "Sit down, LaFontaine," he said and motioned to a chair. Jack took the chair, but sat on the edge of it rigidlly. The colonel looked up and smiled. "Lieutenant, at ease, man. If you fell off that chair, you'd break." Jack consciously loosened his body and the colonel leaned back in his chair. "Jack, I'll give it to you straight. You come with a great record. You are a fine pilot, you're young, you're intelligent, you're eager, all qualities I need in a man for a mission coming up." Jack grew quiet, as did the colonel. "It's vital to our plans, but it is as dangerous as hell, Jack and I won't order any man into it. I want a volunteer. Now, before you say anything, I've got to tell you this----you go in with no identification, so if you are killed or captured you cannot be traced back to England. The details are tedious and I will spare you, but suffice it to say, there would be terrible reprecussions. Are you interested?" John thought for a minute. If it weren't for Anne, he wouldn't even have to think, but he was an Army pilot and this is what he signed up for. "Yes sir, very interested. When would this take place?" "You'll be briefed tomorrow and leave tomorrow night. We don't want too much time to elapse before the actual mission. See you tomorrow at 1300. Get a good night's sleep. It may be your last for a while." Jack stood and saluted. "Yes sir," he said and left the office. His heart was beating wildly. Was it fear or excitement or a little of both?

"I don't even know what my father looked like. Did he look like me or do I look like him, I should say?" Anne sighed. "I wish I still had the pictures of him. I left all the pictures of Jack and me at Mom and Dad's house after Luke and I married and then they had that flood in their basement. Almost everything they had stored for me was ruined. But you have your fathers's mouth, chin and hair and my eyes." "Did Dad know about the pictures that got ruined in the flood?" She smiled. "Oh, I think he suspected. Your father never asked me for that piece of my heart that I had given away forever, just the part for him. Your father was a wise and loving man and my life was very rich with him. I have to know that the Lord knows what will happen and wants the best for everyone." John looked up at his mother. "Mom, don't ask to go with me. I really don't know if you could handle the trip. I love you and I want to keep you forever." Anne looked at him and smiled. "Honey, when I was 25 years younger than you are now, my Daddy died and then Mama the next year. You don't keep anyone forever. I need this trip as much as you do." John looked at his mother and for the first time, realized what his Dad must have gone through, trying to live with that subborness. Dad saw much more positive than negative and so did he. He realized, for the first time, that his mother was her own woman, a strong individual in her own right, and he chuckled. "Mom, I couldn't think of anyone I would rather have along than you."

Jolene and Bill were beside themselves, realizing that John was only a half brother. Jolene thought for sure if anyone was a half brother, it would have been Bill, because didn't Jolene and John both start with J? And wasn't Bill the odd duck out? What's the deal here? John chuckled and said there was no accouting for wierdness and Bill hit him in the arm, just like when they were kids. John bit back tears when Jolene flung her arms around her neck and said nothing had changed, he was still her superduper calioususexpialidousous big brother! (what she used to call him when they were kids.) And Bill, hitting him in the arm again (he was getting a little tired of this term of endearment) said there was no greater big brother and he could give a flying truck whose parentage was who, because as far as he was concerned, they all shared the same Mom and Dad. Anne watched them, remembering how close they had all been as kids. Jolene and John had formed a dynamic duo and then Bill had come along and been, as Jolene said, "the odd duck out". They could tease and torment their little brother but let someone else do or say anything against Bill and Jolene and John were a force to be reckoned with! While John and Jolene had found their niches in high school, Bill had never had many friends. John, sensing Bill's pain, became his champion and friend and the brothers were still close. And the many times, being the jock in the family, John would shoot baskets or play catch or toss a football with his brother so Bill could make a team, did not go unnoticed by Anne. Bill just didn't have the athletic prowess John did, but he knew his way around a hammer and saw and neither John or Luke were very handy with tools. Jolene, being the only girl was loved, petted and tormented by both of them. For instance the time when Jolene got her first bra and John gave it to Bill and told him it was a slingshot. Jolene was mortified when she discovered her new "Teen Bra" hanging on a limb of the big apple tree in the front yard. Luke made a show out of yelling at them, but Anne suspected he secretly thought it was hilarious. However, Jolene was his only girl and as far as he was concerned, the boys should be her protectors. They grew up so quickly and soon only Bill was left in high school, a lonely sceptre without his brother and sister. Anne shook the memories from her head and turned back to the conversation among her children. John was grateful for this loving support, but he did explain that he had to know what had happened to his biological father. They understood, but did express concern about Mom going on the trip. It was out of the question that either of them should go, as they both had jobs, Jolene as a caseworker with Social Services and Bill his own construction company and they could not leave either job for any length of time. Mom and John were planning to be gone for a month. But after dinner and conversation, everyone understood the need and tears and hugs and affirmation and prayer together cemented the trip. John needed to speak with his children and he did, his daughter understanding immediately, his son not so quick. "Grandma is too old for this trip. Why would you do this to her?" Whereas, John protested that Grandma insisted on going and he should talk with her. And so Luke (named for his grandfather) had approached his grandmother in his young man arrogant manner, demanding that she stop this nonense. And Anne smiled at her grandson, whom she loved so, and touched his cheek and told him he didn't make decisions for her and hadn't she changed his diapers and knew all his foibles and childish ways? And he sputtered and protested and she laughed and told him what a great adventure it would be and he was finally seated at her kitchen table eating apple pie and nodding as she explained why she and his father had to do this. And so it was that the whole family was at the airport (not the train station like so many years ago) still supporting each other, still loving each other and seeing off John and Anne as they boarded the plane to France.

Anne feigned sleep as the plane ascended into the air. She thought what Jack must have thought so many years ago. Here I go, and I do not know what I will find. Oh, Luke, I have loved you all these years, do not deny me this time with Jack to close our life together. And immediately a peace that surpasses all human understanding overcame her and she knew where it came from. She dozed then, gently venturing into the life that had been her's and Jack's so many years ago, before the blow and the devastation hit her life. Such a short time, but so much love. The plans they had made. He would forever be that 21 year old boy, while Luke had aged as she did, right along with her. She hoped his end had been peaceful. She had never been able to dwell on that. He had told her he "was not a religious man" and neither had she been at the time, but Luke had been a devout Christian and over the year that they had seen each other. she too had found the Lord as her Saviour. Oh, the joy of that day. She smiled thinking of it and then quickly it left her face. Had Jack found the Lord before he went down? Did he know the peace that passes all understanding too? Oh, she hoped so. She had prayed many times that prayer and she hoped the Lord had answered before she even knew to pray it.

May 26, 1944 Jack

Jack had checked the instruments for the last time. There was no more he could do. This was it. He was to fly to France, not Germany, as the rumor had it. It was to be an intelligence mission to prepare for the much bigger mission that was coming up. He wanted to do well. None of the guys had asked him any details. They had just slapped his back and made crude jokes and tried to give him extra cigarrettes, even though he had never smoked. He had taken them because he knew they meant well by it and he could always use them to trade. He was one of the few people he knew that didn't smoke and Europeans smoked even more than Americans, if that was possible! He touched his wedding band that was on a chain around his neck. At first they weren't going to let him take it, but after examining it, they told him he could put it on his dogtag chain and leave the dogtags behind. No identification. All he had was a comb, a handkerchief and his wedding ring. His buddies had given him a thumbs up and he swallowed a lump in his throat. In a pretty short time he had made some close friends and he knew good and well he may never see them again. But I will, he had resolved, I promised I'd come back to you, Anne, and I will. We are going to have fun making those six kids! And he had smiled at the thought. The flag had dropped and he pushed the throttle. Everything had gone well up until this point and now, from a German ship, he had taken fire. It didn't seem too bad at first, but he was now at the point that he wasn't sure he could make land. He was slowly losing altitude, his ship was dying inch by inch. He always thought if you went down, it was in a blaze of glory, but he was still over water. The plane gave a sputter, just as he spied land and started to dive. "Please God," he prayed. "Help me. Oh, Anne, oh, Baby, I'm sorry. I tried. Oh, Anne, Oh God."

She heard her son stirring next to her and she lifted her head and opened her eyes. He smiled at her, patting her hand. "Doing alright, Mom?" he asked. She laughed. "Always the worrier. I'm fine, honey. I just dozed for a minute and a woman my age has that right, you know!" She also did not like flying that much. Oh, it was much better than when Luke and she had flown to California for a reunion of his service buddies in 1955, howbeit, there was a little less legroom now. But everything felt much more stable and she knew that the airlines had been in business for more than just a few years! John shook his head. "I guess I am just a little nervous. I don't really have the faintest idea where to start, except what the War Dept told us about where he was supposed to have gone down. I'm glad we took a month, although I know we both hate to be away from our grandchildren that long." Anne looked at him fondly. "Yeah, the heck with the children. I remember when Jolene and Ken were stationed in Japan for 3 years and then extended for another 3 with OUR grandchildren. When they finally got home, I went right for the grandchildren, leaving Jolene and Ken in the dust." She thought fondly of Jolene's 3 boys, who were stairsteps, all born in Japan. And John had a boy and a girl, Amanda named after Cathy's mother and Luke, named after John's father. And then there was Bill, named after Anne's brother Billy, who had died in Korea. Anne shook her head. He never could live up to the golden boy his big brother had been, not that anyone ever expected him to be anything other than himself. Luke had favored John a bit, probably so as not to favor his biological children over him. It didn't hurt Jolene because she was the only girl and had her own place, but Bill had suffered a bit. John was a great big brother though, taking him under his wing, making sure he was well taken care of. Oh, Luke had not neglected Bill or ignored him or even remotely acted like he was not as important to him as the rest of the kids, but something in his manner showed Bill he would never measure up and it had hurt Anne as she watched it over the years. Recently, father and son had become closer, perhaps the years filling in the space that had kept them at arms length. And then Bill made a name for himself in town and the neighboring areas with his good quality and honest work in his construction company. Luke was proud of him and started praising him for his honesty and good workmanship and finally, they had settled into a warmer relationship that worked for them both. Then, suddenly, Luke was gone. Bill had never had any children and had been married 3 times. Right now he was dating a woman who wanted to take it very slow and Bill seemed very happy with her. She lived in her own house and he in his. She had two grown children and 3 grandchildren and sometimes you would see Bill and Patty with her grandchildren. Yes, Bill was finally getting settled at 61 years old. The flight attendant was coming down the aisle with drinks and Anne and John straightened up and released their tray tables. She looked at her watch. They had 4 hours to go before they were in New York.

Getting off of Air France and into the Charles De Gaulle Airport in Paris, France was a huge deal. Suitcases were being swung from above like a scythe in the air and John was patient enough with her to allow her to sit until the crowd got through the door of the plane. Finally, everyone had gone but them and John stood to take down their carryon luggage. "Ready, Mom?" he asked, extending his hand to her. She took it and pulled herself up. "Thanks for waiting, honey, I was afraid I would get knocked over." "Well, Mom if you would have let me get you a wheelchair, we could have gotten off first!" John replied, a little exasperated. She just looked up at him innocently and he smiled. "Come on, Mom. I should know by now how you are. Putting you in a wheelchair would be like putting socks on a duck!" He shook his head and carrying the suitcases, he ushered his mother off the plane. Anne thought the airport would be a nightmare to navigate, but she was wrong. On the contrary, they had their licenses, passports and visas ready and had nothing to declare, so they were ushered to the "green channel". Anne and John could not believe that it was so easy, as they had heard nightmarish stories of travel abroad and trying to get through immigration and then customs. John had used his smartphone to plan the whole trip and it had worked beautifully. He even had a translator on that thing. She was proud to have a son who was so capable and kind. He had rented a car with the phone and in just a short while they were sitting in a late model Renault with the steering wheel on the wrong side. Anne giggled, it felt so strange and then she and John were laughing heartily like a couple of kids. It felt good.

Driving west from Paris to the coast of Normandy proved to be a lovely scenic trip. There were flat plains, changing to rolling hills that were broken up by forest covered hills and plateaus. Anne exclaimed over the ancient rocky ridges resembling the upturned edge of a huge saucer. The view gave way, eventually to apple orchards that dotted the countryside, dairy farms and grasslands. Thick hedges separated field from field. They deviated south so that they could visit Omaha Beach Memorial. There was still quite a bit of daylight, it being early afternoon. The sight was overwhelming! On a bluff overlooking Omaha Beach, lay a cemetary on 172 acres of a "perpetual concession" land given by the French government. It was the resting place of 9,387 Americans, including men shot down over France in the Army Air Corps, Anne read. Although there was so much to see, including Theodore Roosevelt's two sons, Theodore Jr, killed in WWII and Quentin, killed in WWI, John was more interested in looking at the names of sercvicemen who could not be located or identified. These names were inscribed on the walls of a semicircular garden on the east side of the memorial. This part consisted of a semicircular colonnade. A huge bronze statue, entitled

"The Spirit of American Youth Rising from the Waves", completed the picture. Facing west was a reflecting pool, burial areas to either side and a circular chapel. John searched the wall, but he soon realized that the unknowns were dedicated to the men who had invaded Normandy on D-Day. Jack had disappeared at least a couple of weeks prior to that. Nonetheless, it was fascinating and they looked around a couple of hours, taking in the rich history. Reluctantly, they climbed back into the Renault and headed toward Cherbourg. Driving up the coast, they were surprised to see mostly sandy shore, but it abruptly turned rugged, howbeit, still beautiful, as they neared Cherbourg. It was the biggest town they had seen since Paris and they quickly found a hotel, as it was almost 8 pm. The hotel had a decent dining room and they ate a quick meal before retiring to their rooms. They were so tired, they couldn't even appreciate the lovely furnishings, but they loved the comfortable beds. At 9 am, they were in the car and traveling to the first small town on their list. These were John's calculations of where his father might have crashed his plane.

The first door they knocked on opened quickly. A small girl, perhaps 4 or 5, gazed up at them. "Is your mama or papa home?" John asked in halting French, studying with his Rosetta Stone as soon as he knew they would be coming to France. She looked quizzedly at them for a moment and then promptly turned and ran back into the house. In a moment, a woman of about 30 years old stood in front of them. "We have come to inquire of Jacques LaFontaine. He was a pilot in WWII and his plane would have gone down around here." The woman looked puzzled and then shook her head. "No, no Jacques here. Goodbye." She shut the door, albeit politely, in their faces. John sighed. "I do not think this will be easy. That woman looked at me like I was crazier than a bedbug!" Anne smiled. That had been one of Luke's favorite expressions, "crazier than a bedbug!" Luke was so much a part of John, yet John did have inborn mannerisms of his father, Jack, such as the laughter, unique and smooth as water. Anne had never heard laughter like Jack's until John had become a teenager and his little boy laugh suddenly became his father's. It had startled her and thrown her into a panic everytime she heard it until finally, she relaxed and learned to love the fact that John had, indeed, something of his father's.

"Look Mom, I'm starving, let's find someplace to eat." said John. Anne shaded her eyes with her hand looking around the street on which they were standing. "Honey, I am not sure there is a restaurant in this tiny village. Why don't we ask?" So they went down the street a couple of doors and tried their luck at a bright red door on a little yellow house. John looked at his mother, shrugged his shoulders, and knocked at the crimson door. Nothing happened, so he knocked again. Still no one answered his summons. "I am afraid no one is home here, Mom," he stated and just as they were preparing to walk away, a woman came from the back of the house. "Bonjour. How may I help you?" Her English was poor, but understandable and they were happy to hear it. "Yes, bonjour, we are looking for a man, Jacques LaFontaine, a man who might have crashed in a plane in WWII?" Anne looked askance at her son and the French woman looked very puzzled. "WWII? Very few men left from then. Maybe old Etienne Beaulieu. Down the street." She pointed to her left and then also shut the door. "Very friendly town," John snorted derisively. Anne chuckled. "John, they probably think we are crazy, two well dressed Americans coming up to their doors and asking them stupid questions. What would you think if the situation was reversed?" John looked at her and smiled. "Point taken. Well, let's see if we can find this Etienne guy and see if he knows anything about 70 years ago!" They walked up the street, asking various people about Etienne Beaulieu until finally a little boy pointed to a house. "Grandpere Beaulieu!" he said triumphantly. "Do you suppose it's his grandfather?" John asked. "Could be," replied Anne, "or it could be just a respectful name that the youngsters call old people too!" John walked confidently to the door and knocked. A young man answered the door and looked John up and down. "Oui?" he inquired. John cleared his throat and started his spiel. "We are looking for a man, Jacques LaFontaine. He would have been an American pilot who crashed here in World War II." "Deux? Grandpere! Veni ici! Un crazy American de vous voir!" (Two? Grandpa, come here! A crazy American to see you!")John and Anne pretty much understood what he said in any language. An aged man finally appeared at the door. "Oui, comment puis-je vous aider?" (Yes, how can I help you?) Taking a deep breath, John said in halting French. "I am sorry to bother you, but we are on a quest for my father. He was an American pilot who crashed here in WWII, but nobody seems to know what happened to him. The Army and his friends came over, but nobody knew. We thought, perhaps, you might have known or heard something about this when it happened." The old man smiled. "Speak some English. Americans were good to us and we want to be able to talk to them. I sorry about your papa, but I cannot help. Many fliers went down, many plane crash, many men die. Resistance strong in France, many friends die. Too old, too long ago. Sorry." He shook his head and made a gesture with his hand that he was done. His grandson came and put his arm around his shoulder. "No more, Grandpere is tired. Sorry." He gently shut the door and Anne and John were again left on the outside. "We never did ask about a restaurant," Anne mused. John laughed. "Oh, Mom, I don't know how you stay so tiny with that appetite of yours. Let's go check it out."

Sitting in the local pub up the street, John and Anne drank stong coffee and ate meat and cheese on croissants. Everyone had stared as they entered, but then had turned back to whatever they were doing and now the buzz of voices was constant. Anne enjoyed the lilting of the French voices, the laughter, the smiles. John, however was pulling out his smart phone looking at all the data he had collected concerning his father in the past few months. "See Mom", he said, "Jack was last seen taking off from this base and he was supposed to fly here. This was his target." He pointed to a tiny line on his phone which meant nothing to Anne. "And where is that, dear?" she asked patiently. "Well, it's about 20-25 miles away from here. The idea is that he veered off course, was shot down or ran out of gas and crashed within a 25 mile radius. This town is one of 6 tiny villages in that perimeter. I was thinking if we visited all of them, then went back again to the most promising, we might be able to put together what happened to him. I know there were a few men that were never found, probably a whole lot more than we even realize, but I want to satisfy myself that he died. I want to know if someone helped him if he lived, if they buried him if he died. I have a feeling inside that these remote little villages know a lot more than they are telling. They did not fare well in that War. The Germans made an example out of these places, killing their people, taking what little they had. They wiped out one whole village. I think these people laid really low and under the radar as much as they could. Old Etienne mentioned the Resistance. I wonder how involved those towns were in the Resistance." John started punching buttons in his smart phone again and Anne let her eyes wander the room. Two working men (one could tell by their clothes) were sitting at a table with 2 mugs that looked to be ale and big bowls of soup or stew in front of them. Large slices of bread sat on a plate in the middle of the table and it seemed as though they laughed after every sentence. Anne couldn't help but smile at them. She surmised it was the only place in town to gather, because men, women and children were all in there eating and some just visiting. The young waitress who had taken their order came over to their table. "Will there be any more, Madame, Monsiuer?" she asked, proud of herself, because she hadn't spoken any English when she took their order. She laughed at their bemused expressions and pointed to a table by the wall. "Pere anglais", she said. The man waved his hand, got up from his chair and proceeded to come over to them. The priest's face was disfigured by scars on the left side of his face. His eye was almost untouched and it appeared that he still had full vision, however, his mouth and nose had, perhaps, burn scars, but they were so old Anne couldn't tell for sure. John stood in the prescence of the ancient priest, but he waved him down. "Sit my boy, sit, and if I may, I will sit with you," he smiled, pulling a chair from the next table. "How do you do, Sir? Your English is very good," John greeted him. In fact, his accent was very heavy and Anne had a hard time understanding him. "I am understanding you are seeking your father, Etienne's grandson told me. Perhaps I can help you. I was a young man in the war, perhaps 20,21. I don't remember much, my mind was compromised, but I will try to help." He smiled benignly at them, almost as if he didn't quite comprehend why he was talking with them. John was ecstatic. "Father, if you could help us, that would be wonderful! My father's name was Jack LaFontaine and he was an American Army Air pilot. We think he crashed within a 25 mile radius of your village and we wanted to find out if anyone knew him or knew about what happened to him. Was he alive when he crashed, was he dead? Did someone bury him?" John paused for breath, expectation on his face. The priest looked at John with compassion. "It is hard not to want to know what happened to your father, but as I say, my memory was compromised." Seeing John's downcast face, he added, "But I will try to help you. Almost everyone will talk with me, so if you like, we can meet here tomorrow morning and I will go with you to speak with some citizens who may know something. Would that be, uh, how I say, okay?" The priest beamed at being able to pull the American slang out of the air and Anne and John laughed. "Yes, that would be okay, Father. What is your name? I mean, I know you are called Father, but what is your real name?" John inquired. "My given name was Jacques Manet, like the artist. Probably he was a relative of mine, who knows?" He smiled again, that sweet, vague smile and pushed himself up from the table. "So, 8:00 am, is that too early, Madame?" He addressed himself to Anne and she smiled. "Actually, Father, I am the early riser. It is John who sleeps in. And, Father, I am Anne". "It my extreme pleasure to make your acquaintances. I shall see you here at 8:00am tomorrow morning, okay?". And so it was agreed. They had a guide.

Their guide had directed them to a woman in town who had a bed and breakfast of sorts. She rented out rooms by the week and she would feed you meals for extra money, but you had to pay in advance, so John paid for a week for the room rental and breakfast. They figured they did not know where they would be in town all day and would eat where they were. "For a fee", said Madame Chevereaux, "I will pack you both a lunch and will throw in Father's lunch for free". She then made the sign of the cross and John accepted her offer, taking out more Euros to satisfy her pockebook. She had gallantly offered them supper that night, free of charge, and they ate soup, fish and bread which, they discovered, the French considered supper. Dinner was the big meal, at noon, but supper was the light repast at night. Now they relaxed in their sitting room which sat in the middle of their two adjoining bedrooms, with a door to either bedroom from the sitting room. The only way out was a single door from the sitting room that opened into the hallway. Actually, it was a very pretty living quarters. Anne's room consisted of a double bed (nothing like the queen or king sized back home) with a beautiful lace bedspread in roses and greens. A comfortable rocking chair (of which Madame Chevereaux was very proud "It came all the way from America"), an antique dressing table and chest of drawers and pastoral pictures of the French countryside. She had toured John's room, oohing and ahing at the lovely wood in the headboard of the bed, the deep blues and browns that made up the wallpaper and trim and the lovely handmade rug in the middle of the room. She also had a handmade rug in the middle of her room of greens and rose. A modern bathroom had been installed just 6 years ago (thank God, John said), however it was across the hall and was shared by all the guests on the floor, of which consisted of only her and John at this time. John wanted to set a strategy for the following day and Anne listened patiently. "So Mom, if we go up each street and hit each house that Father thinks might have some intel, we could probably canvas half the town by noon," John said excitedly. Anne shook her head. "Intel, John? Really, we aren't on a secret mission. Why don't we just let Father Jacques take the lead? He knows these people and their ways. I think we might just scare them and offend them with our forward ways," Anne replied. John looked at his mother. She was a wise old bird. What she meant was he was being an Ugly American and his mom was trying to slow him down. "You are right again, Mom. It's just that I am so anxious to find out anything at all, just one piece of information about Jack". He sighed, sat down and put his arms on his knees. "I can't believe that six months ago I did not know this man existed and now this is so important to me. Maybe if Dad was still alive it wouldn't be that important, but I don't know....." His voice trailed off and he put his head in his hands. "John, we are tired. We have only been in this country two days and we are still jet lagged. Let's go to bed so we can get up tomorrow and be fresh to go hunting with Father Jacques." John looked at his Mom and smiled. "I guess I will always need my mommy right, Mom?" She gave him a hug. "Darn tootin' and don't you forget it. Goodnight, Son," she said turning to head for the bedroom. "Sleep well". "You too, Mom, goodnight". And they went to their respective rooms and slept like proverbial logs.

At precisely 7:55 am, John and Anne were at the pub that they had been at the day before for lunch. Madame Chevereaux, true to her word, had fed them a huge breakfast at 7 am and so much coffee they felt like they were floating. Father Jacques was walking up the street in the wake of several children who were trying to hold his hand (about 5 already were) or his frock or, in the case of one tiny girl, his leg. He stopped, laughed and picked the child up in his arms. One child shouted something to him in French and with a very dramatic face, he spoke as if he was telling a story. Anne mentioned this to John. "He is Mom, John replied. "I think he is telling Puss and Boots, but I can't be sure. That Rosetta Stone was pretty good, though. I understand a lot." Father Jacques was still laughing and carrying on as he neared the pub. He looked up and saw John and Anne standing there smiling. "Bonjour Anne and Jean!" he called, waving. He said something to the children and they quieted down and stood respectfully at his side. "These are the youngest of my flock," Father Jacques smiled, indicating the children. He kissed the child in his arms and gave her to one of the older girls. "Children," he said in French, "I must take these nice Americans on a tour. Go home now or go play. I will finish the story tomorrow morning. Go now, shoo." And he waved his arms toward them and the children scampered off giggling and singing and calling good bye to their village priest. He turned to them smiling. "Now, I have been thinking who we could speak with and I think I know. Jean Paul Genet is the village historian of sorts. He keeps, how I say it, accounts of the years past. He has a library in the back of his house of happenings in this town from long ago. He lives right down here." He pointed to the left and the three started walking down the street. "The people here are very friendly, but they are quite suspicious of strangers because we don't have many. I doubt anyone would talk to you about anything you really wanted to know because they would be afraid you would bring reporters and attention to this village. Some of the young people are restless and want something different and many have gone to Paris and some of the bigger cities, but mostly we are content in our smallness and family like warmth. Come, here is where Jean Paul and his wife Claudia live." He stopped in front of a rundown looking house with a bright blue door. The French did have a thing about brightly colored doors, at least in this village. Before he could knock, the door was opened by a very attractive 50ish woman, dressed in slacks and a blouse. "Father, commet allez vous!" She looked quizzedly at his two companions and he smiled at her. "Claudia", he explained in French," these are two Americans on a mission. The gentleman's father was mising in action in WWII and he thinks he might have come here. Would Jean Paul be home so we might talk to him about the big War?" Claudia looked suspiciously at them and then back to her priest. She shrugged her shoulders and opened the door wider. "Entre, sil vous plait", she said, inviting them in. "Jean Paul!" she called and then went to the back of the house. Father Jacques looked at them and smiled. Eventually, a short stout gentleman with a distracted look came from the back of the house. "Father Jacques, how good to see you. Americans?" he asked, indicating John and Anne. "Yes, they are looking for this gentleman's father. He was an American Army Air pilot in the big war. He was shot down in this area, maybe 25 miles away, at least that is what the American Army told these people. The lady is his widow." He smiled at Anne. She felt like a fraud, since she had been married over 60 years to Luke. He was speaking in English so Anne suspected that Jean Paul spoke English also. She was right. "Please to come in and sit in chairs," he invited in heavily accented and stilted English. But his smile was genuine and his eyes kind and Anne relaxed visably. "Please to introduce to you, John LaFontaine and Mrs. Anne LaFontaine", Father Jacques said, sweeping his arm to them. John spoke up. "I can understand how you could make that mistake, but my stepfather adopted me 65 years ago and I became John Crawford and my mother is Anne Crawford." John surprised himself at how fiercely he protected his name. Yes, he wanted to find out about his father, but he would always be Luke Crawford's son, John. "Forgive me, my mistake. I did not realize," Father amended, but something closed in his face and in Jean Paul's face also. Then both men smiled and sat down. "Now, there were many fliers that went down, but not around here that I know of," Jean Paul said. "Mostly French Resistance came here, we hid them or rather, the people that lived here then hid them.

You must understand, people did not talk. Lives depended on secrecy and that is how these people lived. Even now, it is hard to find anyone who lived through the war who wants to talk about it. Old Etienne Beaulieu, he had a hard time. We never knew what happened. And Father here, it is rumored he was in the Resistance, but even he does not remember it. Much pain for the people who went through this, so much, they block it out. Well, they say Father was brainwashed, but no one who lived at that time knows for sure. They will only say friends rescued him from torture before they could kill him. Very brave men. Most dead now. No, I am sorry. Not much information about that war. Sad, so sad." He shook his head like old Etienne had and stood up indicating this meeting was over. "I will ask around and if I find anything, I will let you know." He smiled at them and put out his hand, but both Anne and John knew that he had shut them out when they mentioned Anne had remarried and John had taken his stepfather's name. Anne couldn't quite figure out why that made a difference to them, but it was palpable. Anne and John stood and John shook his hand. "Well, thank you Monsieur. We appreciate your time." They nodded at each other and left the house. Everyone was quiet as they walked from the house and then John blurted out, "How come you all shut down when we told you Mom remarried? What was wrong with that?" The priest lifted one eyebrow. "Wrong? Nothing is wrong, but then your allegience belongs to the man who's name you bear. And you dishonor him by coming to find the first man." John shook his head. "There is no dishonor. My stepfather has died. I did not even know he was not my father until after he died. I loved him, he treated me like his son. He was a good man, but I never knew the first man. I would like to know him." John looked at the priest's stony face and tried again. "I don't understand why looking for my biological father is dishonest. We want to know that this man was cared for if he lived, buried when he died. My mother has lived all these years not knowing what happened to her husband. She was 17 years old when he died and pregnant with me. Should she live like a nun all her life and mourn for a man who is dead? Is that a good way to raise a child? Or should she live again and give her child a father?" John shook his head. "I don't understand." They walked in silence for a while longer and then Anne spoke. "Father, I loved my husband very much. When he died, I wanted to die. It was only the fact that I found out I was pregnant that I began to eat again. I had to live for Jack's child if nothing else. I never thought I would love again. And then Luke came into my life and he and John connected right away and I had never seen John so happy. He had an uncle and a grandfather, but that is not the same as having a father. I did not marry again until after I knew there was no hope I would ever see Jack again. It was a pain I almost could not bear and I never told John until a few months ago. Do you think I did not love my husband? No, it was the opposite. I loved him so much that I wanted his son to have the best life I could give him. And he did, Father Jacques. And I will not apologize for being married to a loving, kind man who took another man's son as his own. And if Jack knew, I am sure he would approve. How dare you sit in judgement of me when you have never had children or ever married? You don't know what it is like." Anne had run out of steam and thought she better stop before she started to cry. They were back at the pub and sat down at an outside table. "And you, my dear Anne, do not judge me, as you do not know why I didn't marry or why I knew God called me to this life. We will forgive each other our misunderstandings, no, and be friends again, yes?" Anne looked at him for a few moments, her indignation fading and smiled. "Of course, Father." "Good! Tomorrow I will take you to my best friend, Rene Mirabeau, who was in the Resistance with me. What is strange, neither of us remember it! But I am sure you will be welcomed by him and his lovely wife Charlotte and their six children! Well, the children do not live there anymore, but there is always one or two there or one of the 17 grandchildren! Or possibly great grandchildren. I did not count how many of them they have!" His eyes twinkled and Anne felt like they had the old Jacques back. "That would be good, Father. I would like to meet your best friend. Do you think he would remember anything?" John asked. Father Jacques shook his head. "I doubt it. Rene's memory is worse than mine. As you Americans say, like swiss cheese! Anyhow, we will be welcomed and perhaps Charlotte can answer your questions." He smiled at them and stood to leave. "Believe it or not, I do actually work and much awaits me at my church. Tomorrow again at 8:00 am?" They agreed and the priest walked away to his church. "Well, we still have Madame Chevaneaux's lunches and Father Jacques' too. I forgot to give it to him. Why don't we take a ride in the countryside or to the next town and see what we can find out. What do you say?" John asked. "Well, that sounds lovely. Let's do it," Anne answered.

An hour later, they stopped the Renault in front of what looked like a beautiful park. A plain unadorned white cross stood under an enormous tree about 100 feet back from the road. John and Anne got out and made a beeline to the cross. It read "Au Soldat Inconnu". Quickly John consulted his smart phone translator. "To the Unknown Soldier. I wonder if that means for all the wars and all soldiers or just for certain wars and French soldiers," John mused. Anne sighed. "I don't know, dear, but let's sit at this table and eat this lunch. There is so much. It would be a shame to let it go to waste." John sat down at the table his mother indicated. Mrs. Cheveneaux had packed meat and cheese and bread, not together but separately. There was also some fruits and vegetables and a delicious looking eclair like dessert. Anne was tempted to skip all the sensible stuff and go right to the good stuff, but she picked up a piece of cheese and started nibbling on it. The landlady had also included a bottle of red wine and a jug of water, along with 3 wine glasses. John smiled. "These French really know how to eat, don't they?" "Well, John, wine is our water to them, so actually she gave us two jugs of water!" They laughed and she poured them each a glass of wine. "Just one for me, Mother, I'm driving", John said. He made a sandwich out of the meat, cheese and bread and stuffed it unceremoniously into his mouth, washing it down with wine. "It's really beautiful here, isn't it?" he said to his mother. Anne surveyed the park. "Yes, it is. Do you think anyone will answer our questions?" she asked him. John took another bite of his sandwich and chewed for while without answering. He was so much like Luke in his mannerisms. He took time to think on her question before answering. He swallowed his sandwich and took a swig of the water that was in the bottle. "Not sure, Mom. You know, I really don't want to leave here without knowing what happened to Jack. I really don't like loose ends." Anne chuckled. "Well, that's the surgeon in you dear." They sat for a while more, visiting, talking about Father Jacques and the people they had met in town while they finished their lunch. Well, ate their fill, because all three lunches put together could have fed 8 people. They gathered up the remains of their lunch and headed for the car or "auto" as the Europeans called it. John opened the car door for his mother and, after helping her in, closed it behind her. He stood beside her door for a moment, thinking. "You know, Mom, I think we should see if this town has a library. It is a little bigger than the town we are staying in, Seaport Vue. What was the name of this town? Did you see a sign?" he asked her. "Jolieville", Anne answered. She looked at her son. "Pretty town?" John straightened up from leaning in her window and said, "Yeah, I think that's what it means. We better get going." He walked around to the driver's side, got in and started the car. "I sure hope this place has a library. I really don't want to go knocking on doors again!" He backed out and started down the street. The town looked to have approximately 8 or 9 streets with perhaps a population of 700-800 people. They really didn't think they would actually find a library, but lo and behold, there it stood right next to the local pub. The sign read "Bibliotheque" (Library). There was a boy with a book reading on one of the outside tables in front of the pub. Again, John parked the car and walked around and opened the door for his mother. He offered his hand, she took it and pulled herself up. "Knees don't fail me now!" she quipped tweaking a line from an old movie. John chuckled and they walked the 6 steps up to the library door. The inside of the library was much more impressive than the outside. There were about 10 shelves filled with books and there were even 2 computers on a table in the front. Even the Librarian had a computer and he smiled at them as they came in. "Bon Tardes, Madame, Monsieur. How may I help you?" he asked in French. "Bon Tardes, Monsieur." John struggled a bit with his French and had to consult his smart phone quite a bit, but he was able to convey that he would like to look at all local history from 1944 to 1946. The librarian led them to a computer. "Newspapers." he explained in English. "France was occupied at that time, so there weren't many French free newspapers", he said in French and then switched to English," but may help, no?" John shook his hand. "Merci, oui. I think that is just what we are looking for." They sat down at the computer. John hit several buttons and the machine jumped into action. "Okay, Mom, this is going to be tedious because it will all be in French and I will have to keep consulting my smart phone, so you might want to just relax." The librarian reappeared with a huge volume entitled, "Local History and Legends" in English. "Anglais, Madame. May help, no?" Anne laughed. It seemed like that was the only English phrase the man knew, but he had gone to the trouble to help and she was grateful. "Merci, Monsieur, may help, yes!" As the librarian walked away, she said to her son, "I will see if I can find anything in this. I don't know where he found this, but it just might have something in it!"

An hour later, they were no further than they had been when they had walked into the library. They decided to call it a day, as they were both stiff from sitting. They walked up to the desk to thank the librarian for his help. His English was not near as bad as they had thought.

"What is it you are looking for exactly. May help, no?" he inquired. Anne stifled a giggle and did not dare look at John. After all, this man was trying to help them! John repeated the story about Jack being shot down and the librarian (Monsieur Claudel they found out) furrowed his brow and thought for a moment. "This bibliotheque is given to us by an American soldier. Every year he sends money for books and two years ago, he sent 3 computers. My grandfather knew him. That is why I am the bibliotheque. My grandfather was first and my father after him and now me. If I ever have a son, I have four daughters, he will be bibliotheque. If I have no son, then whichever one of my daughters is interested." He shrugged as if it was inconsequential. "Did you ever hear of an American flier that crashed here?" John asked. Monsieur Claudel shrugged his shoulders again. "Sorry no. There are many rumors from the big war, but mostly the old people know them. Sorry." He smiled vaguely at them and turned back to his work. "Well, Merci, anyhow," John said, mixing the languages. "Oh, Monsieur," the man said, without looking up. "Perhaps there is something. There is old Claude who lives in the apartment building in town, but he is never there. He walks incessantly around town talking to himself." Noting Anne's startled look, he continued, "Not to worry. He is completely harmless. The nuns watch out for him, making sure he has food and that he goes to sleep at night. He is not completely helpless. He cooks for himself and lives alone. He gets along. But he is about the age of the man you seek." He looked up at them and smiled. "You can just walk up to him and talk to him. He mainly only repeats what you say, but maybe it will help, no?" "Again, merci, monsieur. Uh, is this man an American?" John inquired. Again, Monsieur Claudel shrugged his shoulders, a favorite gesture of his. "No one knows. He only repeats what you say in any language." "Good, thank you sir." They walked along the sidewalk, hoping to spot the man in question, but they only saw people sitting outside of the pub and some children playing on the corner. "You up for a walk, Mom? The town couldn't be that big!" John said. "I would love to stretch my legs. A walk sounds great!" Anne answered. They crossed the street toward the town square and heard a man's booming voice call out, "Bonjour Claude", followed by several children's voices calling, "Bonjour Monsieur Claude!" They looked up to see a bearded, long haired man walking with a determined stride, head down, ignoring the calls. Anne and John hurried to catch up with him. John reached him first, touching his shoulder. "Bonjour Claude," he said, trying to get the man to look at him. Claude slowed down at the touch and looked at John, staring at his face. Anne finally caught up with them. "What do you think Mom? Could this be him?" Anne looked at the hirsuite face, the lonely haunted eyes and wanted to cry. "I don't know, John. Jack, it's Anne." She addressed old Claude by the name of her first husband and Claude turned his gaze to her. "Anne, Anne, Annie", he replied in a singsong voice. Anne started a bit. "What Mom, is there something familiar?" John asked, noticing her response. "I just don't know dear. Jack is the only one who ever called me Annie." Claude again started his singsong conversation. "Anne, Anne, Annie." Anne studied him, trying to find something familiar in this man, but it was almost impossible with the hair and grime. He was still staring at her and he did have the beautiful eyes that Jack had. She was unsure. She just couldn't tell. "I just don't know, dear," she sighed. John made a disappointed noise. "Well, let's find the convent or the nunnery or whatever you call it and talk to the sisters. Maybe they can help. And why the heck didn't Father Jacques mention this guy?" "Probably, he just didn't think of, dear. These towns might be close together for us, but I don't think Father leaves Seaport Vue too much," Anne answered. John went to ask one of the men the way to the convent while Claude stared into Anne's face. "Adieu, Claude," she said quietly. "Adieu Claude, Jack, Jack, Jackie, Anne, Anne, Annie," but he did not move and John came back to stand beside her. "Bonjour, Claude," John said, touching the man's shoulder. Claude looked at John's hand and tears came to his eyes. He turned and walked again on his way. Both John and Anne were very touched by this encounter. They did not know if it was Jack, but they did not know it wasn't him either. Their hearts were seared with the sadness of his situation, whether he was Jack or not. They started for the convent on foot. "It's not that far and we still need to stretch our legs," John said, trying for some normal conversation. Anne nodded, too overcome with emotion to speak. That poor man! That could be her Jack. And if it wasn't, it could be someone else's husband who never came home. She took a deep breath. "You okay, Mom?" Jack asked kindly. "Fine dear. How far is this convent?" "Just two streets over. We should be there shortly." And like a mirage, it popped up before their eyes, an ancient gray stone building with an iron fence around it. They rang the bell that attached high to the fence and in a few moments a nun, still dressed in the old habit, came to greet them. "Bonjour, Madame, Monsieur." She spoke in rapid fire French and even John couldn't follow her. He asked her in French to slow down and she laughed. "I speak some English. Mother taught us. Come in, come in." She opened the gate and led the way inside to a lovely garden. "Shall we sit here? It is a lovely day. I will get Mother. It will only take a moment." And with that, she left with a swish of her robes. Anne thought of Jack with nostalgia, knowing that those robes would bring back childhood memories of the only family he ever knew before her. Presently two nuns emerged, the younger nun that had first greeted them and a much older lady. "This is Mother Superior. Perhaps she can help you." With that, the young nun nodded and left the garden. John had stood when the women approached and now Mother Superior motioned him to sit, as she did. She lifted her old face to them and smiled. "How can I help you?" she asked in accented English, although her English was very understandable. "We would like to inquire about the old man that walks around town, Claude," John started and then proceeded to tell her the story of his father. Mother

Superior listened patiently and smiled. "Yes, dear Claude. Well, he was here before I took my vows. I don't know how he came to be here. I just know the sisters have always watched out for him. He is one of God's children." She smiled benignly at them and John nodded. "But you want to know all I know about Claude, non? You seek your father and you look for him in all faces, non?" She smiled kindly at John and seemed to understand his urgency. "I know Claude was in the war. Do I know if he is American, French, German or Polish? No. Do I know if he is a Jew? No. He could be all or none of these things. I do not know. I just know it is my duty and honor to serve him for Christ. So we take him food and make sure his apartment is clean and clean his clothes. As for cleaning him, well....." She shrugged helplessly and smiled again. "I have been here a long time and Claude was in his 40's or so when I came. He was a nice looking man, but he had facial scars. Something had made him the way he was, maybe torture I don't know. There are so many sad stories. The Lord allows us to bind one another's wounds and that is what we have tried to do for Claude. He doesn't get close to anyone, even children, but he will allow someone to do for him or walk beside him. He only repeats what he hears, although once in a while, I have heard him say something on his own." John sat straight up on the bench. "Like what, Sister?" Mother smiled at him. "Well, he said, "Sister, you are like my mother", but he had heard one of the sisters calling me Mother, so it might have gotten all jumbled up in his mind." Anne's mind was in a turmoil. Sisters were like mothers to Jack. What could this mean, if anything? Suddenly, Mother Superior touched her hand. "My dear, even if Claude is your lost husband, he does not know it. You said you spoke with him? He called you Annie, but he also said Jackie. He is best left here in familiar surroundings where everyone knows and loves him and takes care of him. It is what we do. This is his town." She squeezed Anne's hand and then stood, indicating that the visit was over. "You are most welcome to return and visit Claude at any time, but I think to take him from here would be cruel," Mother Superior stated. Anne and John stood also. "I believe you are correct, Mother. Perhaps we will come again. We just want to find out what happened to Jack. I cannot be sure if Claude is even him." "Of course, I understand. I wish I could be of more assistance, but that is all I know and I believe Claude might be the oldest person in town. All that knew his story are dead. Goodbye and God bless you." And with that, Mother Superior walked them to the gate and they left. Walking down the street back toward the library, they spotted Claude striding along with 2 dogs following. They saw him slip them a treat and John smiled. "Well, he loves dogs and it looks like the feeling is mutual." The dogs skipped around him trying to get his attention, but he kept his eyes on some unknown destination. They finally reached the library and once again, they backed the car out and started out of town. Driving along the country road, Anne remarked about the vegetation and the fact that there was no fencing when suddenly John slammed on his brakes and swerved to the side of the road.. Startled, Anne looked up to see an old farmer driving two or three hogs across the road at a slow pace. One hog had gotten away from him, probably frightened by the car and was running towards them. The old farmer ambled toward them. "Souiee!" the man called and the hog stopped and turned and trotted back to the farmer. He reached down to pet and comfort it, scratching behind the ears. After he was done placating the hog, he walked up to the car, looked in John's window and said, "Monsieur, pour quoi ne vous chase mon porc avec vorte auto? Ils ne sont pas utilises pour cela." John quickly consulted his smart phone. "Oh, no sir, I am not chasing your hogs with my car," he replied in French. "I just did not see them crossing. Je suis desole (I am sorry)". The man smiled. "American accent. I speak Anglais un peu." He stood there with approximately three teeth in his whole mouth, which gave him the look of a scarecrow, what with the hat and the plaid shirt. John soon began telling him of why he was here and the man's face lit up. "Ah, yes, I was a boy, perhaps, 10 years old. I saw a fire in the sky of a plane going down. I went to tell my papa, but he said it was too far away." "But did you hear anything? Were there any survivors?" John asked eagerly. "I don't know. I heard yes, I heard no. I never saw anyone. It was bad crash, lots of fire. But I never heard anything about it. I was a kid and there were so many secrets. Nobody told kids anything because they were afraid if anyone spoke any secrets, the Nazis would come and wipe out our town just like they did with Oradour-sur-Glane. Terrible time. I was just a kid, but I know I saw a plane go down. But nobody talked. Nobody said anything." He shrugged and started back toward his hogs. John looked at this mother. "What do you think? Could that have been Jack? Could it have been Claude?" "I don't know honey. Maybe. But like he said, he was probably 10 years old and it could have been anything. And if it was a plane, nobody is talking," Anne offered. John hit the steering wheel with his hand. "I should have asked him where. Where? At least I could have looked." Anne put her hand gently on his arm. "Honey, I don't think he knew exactly where. He just saw the fire. It could have been anywhere. I bet you could see that fire for 50 miles. Let's get back to Seaport Vue. It's almost 6:00pm. Maybe we can talk Madame Chevereaux into supper, what do you think?" And she gave him her best Mom smile and he capitulated.

The next morning they were at Mrs. Cheveneaux's breakfast table, enjoying what looked like oatmeal but tasted like ambrosia. That woman could cook. She had fed them supper the night before and told them, not so discreetly, that they could leave the money for it on the table. By 8:00 am they were again in front of the pub waiting for Father Jacques. They heard him and his noisy entrouge approaching. Anne looked sideways at John. "A little de je vous?" she asked, "and we are even in the right country". John smiled absent mindedly, his mind on the upcoming meeting. Another man that was his mother's age and Father Jacques' age who might be able to add one more piece to the puzzle. He wanted to question him about the plane that the old man said he saw go down as a child. Someone had to have seen it. Why didn't Father Jacques mention that along with Claude? If the boy, who was now an old man, had seen it, surely most of the people in this area had. He had lots of questions for Father Jacques' friend and for Father Jacques. Around the corner came Father Jacques and his bevy of youthful admirers. This time he was doing a silly walk and John suspected he was showing how Puss in Boots walked in the boots. The children were laughing and boisterous but quieted when they saw John and Anne. Anne, in her grandmotherly wisdom, had brought a bag of candy and started handing it out to the children. "Oh Anne, you will take my place in their affections!" Father laughed good naturedly, as the children clamored for the candy. Many "merci Madame" were heard and finally the candy was gone. "What, none for me?" Father quipped. A little boy shyly held out his candy. "You may have mine, Pere Jacques," he said in French. Father patted his head and gave him a hug. "My good hearted Michel Blain. That is okay my son. Father has many sweets all around him!" And he waved goodbye to the children who promptly took off with their candy. Little Michel Blain turned to wave and ran to catch up with the other children. Turning to Anne and John, Father Jacques asked, "Shall we?" and still chuckling the three new friends started walking. "Rene and Charlotte live right across from my church on the next street," he said. "I would be honored to show you our little church building. The people of the town rebuilt it after the war. It was razed. I only heard that a stray bomb fell and nobody was hurt. I don't remember," he explained, seemingly anticipating their question. They walked as Father Jacques pointed out different homes and said peoples' names they would probably not remember. "Father," John asked. "What do you know of the man Claude in Jolieville?' Father Jacques frowned in thought and then his face cleared. "Ah, you mean, old Claude who walks around the town and repeats what you say? The nuns care for him." "Yes,

yes, that's the one," John said impatiently. "I do not know. Perhaps a Jew who was tortured, perhaps a German who is tortured in his mind by his own crimes. Maybe a Frenchman who saw too much evil and lost his mind. No one knows." "Could he be an American?" John asked. Father looked startled. "Well, I suppose, I never thought of it." He suddenly caught onto what John was getting at and put his hand on John's shoulder. "I do not know if he is your father, John. He could be, he could not be. That is a mystery we shall never unravel. I am sorry." They walked on a bit in silence until they saw the church in the distance and Father Jacques exclaimed, "Here we are! Rene and Charlotte's". They walked up the well kept path with flowers accenting the yard and knocked on a bright yellow door. Anne was getting used to these doors and thought she would miss them when she got back home. The door was immediately opened by a woman around Anne's age. She was lovely still, even though elderly, John thought. She started and then smiled brightly and said, "Oh, Jacques! Rene had to leave suddenly with Henri. They went to the boat to make repairs and see about the catches that just came in." Then remembering her manners, she said, "Oh, please forgive me. Come in, come in. Sit, have some coffee and cake." She smiled and looked to Father Jacques for an explanation. "Charlotte, see how I take the friendship of you and Rene for granted? I bring guests without notice! This is Anne and John Crawford and they come looking for what happened to John's father. I mentioned them to you the other day." Charlotte looked puzzled and then smiled. "Oh, of course, the Americans! Perhaps I can help you with something? I was a teenager and I remember many things. Please to sit down." Charlotte spoke passably good English and seemed to be very nice, but John was disappointed. He had been looking forward to meeting this man. "When will he return?" John asked her. "I am not sure. It depends on the repairs. My husband is an expert repairing boats and Henri, our son-in-law, his boat is in poor shape. They will return as soon as they can." John smiled gamely and said, "Perhaps I would like a piece of that cake." "Of course, Monsieur. And Madame, Jacques, would you like some too? And coffee. How do you take your coffee?" She was babbling, seemingly nervous and Anne took pity on her. "Please call us Anne and John." Anne smiled, immediately warming to this gracious lady. They ate their cake and drank the rich delicioius coffee. "So, Jean, what is is you want to know? Jacques said you seek your father?" John put down his coffee cup. "Yes, Charlotte, I never knew him. His plane went down when Mom was pregnant with me. I would like to know what happened to him is all. Did he die in the crash? Did he suffer? Did someone help him? These are the things I want to know, my mother and I would like to know." Charlotte sat with her hands in her lap. "Jean tells me you had a stepfather and a very fine one. You did not know he was not your father. Much love passed between you. This was a happy house, no?" She looked anxiously at them. Anne admired her soft heart. "Yes, it was a very happy house and John ended up having a brother and a sister also, but it still doesn't negate the fact that he had a father he did not know. There are answers we don't have and that we need to know to ease our hearts. You do understand?" she asked gently. Charlotte studied Anne and looked about to tell her something, but at that moment a younger woman walked into the room. "Mama, ou etes-vous?" She stopped in her tracks when she saw Anne and John. John stood immediately and Father Jacques hid a smile. "Oh, the Americans", she said in English. "How do you do?" Her English wasn't half bad and John was charmed. She dimpled as she smiled at him. "It is all around town the Americans are here. This is the most excitement to happen in a long time." Anne studied John's face. She hadn't seen him take this much interest in a woman, well, since Cathy. The woman was probably in her early sixties, quite pretty still, very much like her mother and an impish demeanor about her. She looked like someone you should already know. "My daughter, Marie Louise, Marie for short. She is my oldest. This is Anne

Crawford and her son Jean from America." Marie dropped a quick curtsy and then came forward and held out her hand. "Very nice to make your acquaintance. Do I say this correct? I do not get to use my English very much. I like very much to speak it more." John did not know what was wrong with him. This woman was absolutely captivating. He cleared his throat. "So nice to meet you. Do you and your husband live nearby?" Oh, subtle, boy, subtle. They probably did and they probably had a boatload of kids. "I am a widow, Monsieur and I live just down the street." "Oh, forgive me Madame, I was not very tactful. My condolences." She laughed, a tinkling laugh. "Not to worry, Monsieur. And I am Marie and you are Jean, no?" John smiled. "Yes, merci, that's good." Marie sat down at the table and so did John. "My husband died forty years ago when I was twenty-four years old. I have one son and one daughter and that is all. I am content as I am." John laughed. "You have described my circumstances also. I am also widowed for forty years and have one son and one daughter. What are the chances?" She smiled at him and said, "I have never thought about it", and they both laughed, although it wasn't that funny. "Marie, take Jean to the garden and I will visit with Anne. Perhaps we will get more accomplished just the two of us." Anne almost laughed aloud at the way John jumped up and pulled out her chair. They walked out the door talking and smiling at each other. "And I too must be off," Father Jacques said, standing. It is Friday and I must get ready to hear confessions tomorrow and ready the church for mass. Adieu, Anne. I will see you at the church soon, no? Adieu Charlotte." He shook Anne's hand and kissed Charlotte on both cheeks. "Anne, I will not be able to take you around town until Monday I am afraid. Perhaps you can explore on your own, no?" He smiled at her and gave a small salute and walked out the door. Charlotte smiled and said, "Dear Jacques. Between Rene and him, I am run ragged but also well taken care of. They are both such good men. I am afraid they have spoiled all other men for Marie Louise. There were many men interested in Marie after Phillipe died, but she would have none of it. Phillipe was a difficult man and Marie was not anxious to jump so quick back into the lion's den. Now it has been 40 years and she still has not jumped! She says she is content and I think I believe her." Anne nodded her head. "Yes, same with John, but he was so grief stricken overy Cathy I feared for him. If it hadn't been for his children, I don't know what he would have done. Rather like me, when I got the news of my husband almost 70 years ago. If I hadn't been pregnant, I probably would have wasted away. Children can be a real blessing." Charlotte looked at her and then looked quickly away. "Well, I am not sure what to tell you." Anne shifted in her chair and folded her hands on the table. "We were just in Jolieville yesterday and met a farmer there. He told us an interesting story of when he was a boy and saw a plane go down near there, a ball of fire, he said. Do you remember anything like that?" Charlotte got out of her chair. "Let me get the coffeepot and bring it in here," she said and with that, she left the room and went into the kitchen. Anne was a little taken aback by this, but in a few minutes, she returned, smiling, with the coffeepot. "Um, how old was this man when he saw this?" Charlotte asked. "He said he was about 10 years old," Anne answered. "Well, the children, they saw a lot of things they shouldn't have seen and tried to pretend they were more adventurous than they were. Probably, he saw a bomb exploding and thought it more exciting to think he saw a plane. It was a frightening time for all of us, but especially for the children." Anne couldn't shake the feeling that Charlotte was evading her questions. She decided not to tiptoe around and asked her bluntly, "Charlotte, are you trying to evade my questions? Is there something you are not telling me?" Charlotte looked stunned for a moment and then grew redfaced. Finally, she chuckled. "You caught me Anne. I hate to talk about the war. It brings back bad memories. With Father Jacques for example. He almost died. He was Resistance, maybe 20 years old. He got caught on a mission and he was tortured terribly. Some very brave men rescued him at the peril of their lives, my father included. I still don't know how they got him out of there and nobody ever said, but he was never the same after that. He had married shortly before and that was the only thing he did remember, unfortunately, because she only stayed with him for two weeks after that. She had married a dashing exciting Resistance fighter, not a broken quivering boy who could never have children." Charlotte threw her hand over her mouth. "Oh, forgive me, I should not have said that. That was told me in confidence and I have never told anyone." Anne covered Charlotte's hand with her own. "And you still haven't told anyone. I know how you care for Father Jacques. I would never betray that confidence." Charlotte's lip quivered. "You are very kind Anne. I was not prepared to like you so much, but I do." Anne laughed. "And what's wrong with that? I like you too." They laughed together and were still laughing when John and Marie walked in. "What's so funny?" John asked and that sent them into laughter again. Marie and John looked at each other, smiling and shook their heads. "We are just having a good time and that is good, no?" Charlotte said bringing herself under control. "Very bon, Mama, yes good!" Marie said laughing. After they had all had their fill of laughter, they finished the coffee in the pot. "Well, Charlotte, I just wanted to ask you one thing," said John. "Do you think I am a fool to want to know what happened to the man who gave me life? My mother's first love? The man who did not get to raise me because he never came home?" He looked at Charlotte steadily and she seemed very uncomfortable. "Jean, why do you ask me this?" she queried. John sighed. "Because I am beginning to wonder if I am on a fool's errand. I just want to know what happened to him, that's all." Charlotte studied the coffee in her cup and then looked up at John. "No Jean, I do not think you a fool. I think you want to know what happened to your father. But think of it this way. If you never find out, you can imagine anything you want and you can make it very good! That is the best thing about not knowing." She smiled gently at him and then her demeanor changed. "Oh, Jacques wanted you to see his church before the day was out, so perhaps you could go over there now. It is already 10:30 am! Where does the day go?" she said gaily. "Anne, I would like to give you and John a tour of our little town, perhaps, tomorrow when Jacques is busy? Will that be good?" Anne looked at John and he nodded. "Yes, Marie Louise, that would be fine. What time?" Charlotte laughed. "Well, I know that Jacques likes to get up with the sun, but in my old age, I prefer a little later. Is 11:00 am good"? "That's great!" answered John and they all laughed because he was adamant! As they said their goodbyes and left, Anne said to John, "Honey, I am so beat. Could you take me back to the bed and breakfast and then go see Father by yourself. I need a nap". John was immediately solicitous of her. "Mom are you alright? Do you need a doctor? What can I do?" He looked so anxious that Anne laughed. "No I need a nap and you can take me back to Madame Cheveneux's. I am fine, honey, I am just tired. I am 86 years old and you will have to make a few concessions!" So John took her back to their rooms and went to see Father Jacques at his church.

John found the church easily, as it was right across the street from Charlotte's house. Charlotte and Marie were going to walk down the hill to buy fresh bread from the baker, as it was too late in the day to bake it themselves. He entered the small church and found Father Jacques with a dustrag in his hand. "Father, when you said you had to prepare for Saturday and Sunday, I assumed you meant spiritually. I didn't know you had to clean the church by yourself, "John said good naturedly. Father chuckled. "The ladies clean it on Wednesday, but by Friday, it always needs a good dusting again. Come, let me show you our humble church." He stopped short and asked, "Where is your mother?" "She was a bit tired, so she asked if I would give her apologies and went back to the inn to rest." "Ah," Father Jacques said knowingly and walked John around, showing him the small building, 16 pews, 8

49

on each side. At the back of the church stood a confessional, the closet for the priest with two adjoining boxes for the "confessees". When they approached the altar, Father Jacques genuflected and so he did the same, showing respect for the priest's traditions. Finally, they came back down into the church and sat in a pew. "So, my friend, here is where I live my life, worship my God, find my peace. I have been racking my brain to think how I can help you and I think 'Jacques! You can tell all you remember, maybe that will help'. At least, if nothing else, it will give you an idea of how things were back then. So, the first thing I remember of my life is lying on a bed in Richard and Louise's home, Charlotte's parents. Rene was staying there also. Rene, too, had been hurt in the war. He was not strong, but still he took place in the rescue of me. I saw the raw fear in his eyes, the pain, but he conquered it to save me from what had been his fate also. He had escaped earlier than I, but he was always haunted. As I recovered, we talked. I remembered some things, but Rene had shut everything out. He remembered nothing of any torture. I can only imagine it was so horrible that he could not think on it. But I remembered one thing mainly. I had a wife. When I asked where she was, I received only silence. I thought she had been killed, but then Charlotte told me later that she had left. She could not stand to see what had happened to me, so she left before they found me. She was the only reason I held on and then she was gone. Oh, well, I wish her only happiness." He lifted his eyes to John and John saw the pain in there and then calm. "If not for the friendship of Rene and Charlotte and the kindness of the townspeople, I think I would have lost my mind. Strangely, my long term memory was affected and I could not remember much about my childhood. Charlotte told me I was raised in the orphanage in the village by the priest who preceded me. He was killed trying to shield his people." His face grew dark and angry. "That is the first thing the Nazis did to demoralize the people by killing their leaders, especially their spiritual leaders. Charlotte said he was a brave man and we would see him in in heaven. I wish I could remember him." John said gently, "He raised a good and brave man who cares about his flock. That is his legacy to you. Is there still an orphanage in the village?" "Not now. There was for a bit after the war and the women helped look after the children. then when I was stronger, I took my vows, not lightly I assure you, but it was what God wanted and I have been very happy here all these years. And then, those children were mine and I looked after them. Now there is no real need for an orphanage, any orphaned children are usually taken in by relatives. But after the war, oh there were so many!" He looked above John's head as if he was seeing the many children that he had cared for after the war. "Now some of those children are married, some work in the government, one boy even has become rich. Every year at Christmas I recieve a big check to buy gifts for the children of the village and food and we have a big Christmas party in town. The rest goes into a fund in case anyone gets sick and needs a doctor or if someone is hurt and is out of work and can't pay his bills. It is good of Georges to do this, to remember his old Pere and the town that was so good to him." He brought his eyes back to John's. "He lives in Hong Kong now, I think." John rose from the pew and extended his hand to the priest. "Father, thank you so much for showing me your church and Mom and I will see you at Mass on Sunday. Marie told me there was to be a picnic after church Sunday and invited us. I hope that is alright." "Oh, yes, you must come, everyone will be there. It is for all. I will be happy to see you at Mass." He smiled at him with a twinkle in his eye. "I will make Catholics out of you yet, no?" John laughed. "Father, I think you and I are on the same page about the Lord, so I believe we will meet in heaven, Catholic or Protestant. I do not believe either of us are deceived, do you Father?" Jacques laughed heartily. "No Jean, I believe not. Until Sunday then?" "Yes, maybe I can get Madame Chevereaux to make some of her delicious food." Father laughed. "Oh, Marie Fern! She will be there. She is a devout Catholic and she loves to have the best food at the picnic. It is her sin, vanity, but I don't tell her because she makes the best croissants in town!" John chuckled and took his leave of the village priest. There was something about that guy he just couldn't help but like.

The next morning was Saturday and, whether it was force of habit or they were just tired out from their week, both John and Anne slept in until well after 9:00 am, thus missing breakfast. They figured they may as well lounge around in their pajamas for a while and relax. To their surprise, Madame Chevereaux arrived with a coffee thermos, cups and some delicious pastries hot from the oven. Smiling, she put the tray down on the coffee table in the sitting room explaining, "I think you must be tired. Maybe have a tired day today, no?" And with those words, she quietly left the room. John poured Anne and himself a cup of coffee and each took a pastry from the tray. "My goodness, this woman can bake," Anne exclaimed, biting into the warm, sugary concoction and taking a sip of coffee. "Ummmm, I know, really good," John agreed. "Marie Louise said she would take us around town. Do you want to go and visit with Charlotte instead?" Anne thought for a minute. "I guess. I do like her. Maybe she will remember a little bit more about the old days and I can find out something." "Yeah, maybe," John said absent-mindedly. Anne had to smile. He was really liking Marie Louise and she was glad. She had been hoping for 40 years that he would show something more than a passing interest in a woman and he finally had, only 3000 miles from home. Well, whatever, she was glad John was experiencing some romance in his life. They sat and talked for another hour and then got dressed and walked the few blocks to Charlotte's house. It was about 11:00 am. "I will leave you here," John said, giving her a salute. "Marie is just a few houses down." And with that, he walked down the block to pick up Marie for their outing. Charlotte opened the door before Anne could knock. "Oh, I thought I heard voices," she said in her adequate English. "You did. John just went to pick up Marie. I think they were going to sightsee today," Anne answered entering through the door that Charlotte held open. "Not much to see in this small village", Charlotte said. "Jean and Marie seem to like each other, no? Probably they should not get too attached since you are returning to America." Anne looked askance at Charlotte. That was not the first time Charlotte had bordered on rude, but at the same time, Anne had the distinct feeling that Charlotte really liked her. "I hope I haven't come at a bad time. If you prefer, I can go back to the inn." Charlotte turned and put her hands to her face. "Forgive me, dear Anne, I did not mean it like it sounded. Both Jean and Marie are, how you say, kind heart people and I dislike to see them hurt. Both long widowed and now, one lives in America and one in France. I should not think they would be ready to give up their own countries, religion and families and the familiar ways at this stage in their lives. That is all I meant. I would not want to see their hearts hurt." She looked so contrite that Anne touched her arm gently, saying, "Of course, Charlotte, I forget that our languages are sometimes a barrier between us. I know you did not mean anything by that. Forgive me." Charlotte smiled at her. "It is almost dinner time. We shall have a feast, how you say, just us girls, no?" They laughed and Charlotte disappeared into the kitchen and came back with bread, cheese and baked fish. She disappeared again and reappeared with baked carrots and potatoes and a big plate of butter. "I am going to be so big, I am not going to be able to get on the plane!" Charlotte laughed good naturedly and sat down to the table. Both women bowed their heads and Charlotte said the blessing. They talked nonstop through the meal about the town, their children and grandchildren, about neutral topics. "There was a time when every word of that blessing was very heartfelt. We were so hungry all the time." "It must have been very difficult for you," Anne said sympathetically. "How old were you, 14, 15?" "Yes, it wasn't the way I imagined growing up. Anything we grew, the Nazis came in and took and it was rather dangerous to go down and fish at that time. Most of the boys my age were either recruited for the Resistance or the Army." Looking at Anne's shocked face, Charlotte smiled sadly. "The average age for the Resistance was 16, but there were some as young as 14. We were fighting for our lives and it was a desperate fight. Everything was secrecy. There were not very many boys my age in town, so that is why I......" She did not finish the sentence. "That is why you married an older man?" Anne finished for her. "Not so much older, 7 years only, but many men of marriageable age were dead or missing. We married so we could keep on. And it was nice to have someone to care for and care for you. And there was love. I loved Rene. I knew how brave he was, what he must have gone through. And we have been happy," she ended fiercely. "Very, very happy." "I expect you have," Anne countered easily. "And I would love to meet your Rene." Charlotte rose abruptly. "Well, sometimes he is gone for weeks when repairs are to be made. There is a son who lives in that town and Henri and Rene stay with him during this time. It gives him a chance to see the grandchildren." She started to clear the table. "Do you usually go with him to see the grandchildren?" Anne asked. "Sometimes, but Cecile and the children have gone to see her parents in Paris, so it will be just the men. And contrary to what most people think, men do quite well on their own. They will cook their fish and lift their ale and clean the house before Cecile returns and faints at the terrible mess they have made." She laughed. "The men will do quite well without any women or children." Anne smiled also. "I know John has been anxious to meet Rene. Father tells us he remembers nothing of his past life, like himself, which is why they became so close. That and the fact that he recovered at your father's house. But, sometimes, just knowing someone who was around during that era, will spark something in someone's mind. I know that John is not willing to leave until he has some concrete proof of his father's fate, a gravesite, someone who knew what happened to him, something." Charlotte picked up the platter of butter. "I fear Jean will be disappointed. There were too many secrets during the war." She took the butter into the kitchen. Anne picked up the platter of remaining bread and the bowl of carrots and followed her. "Charlotte, is it just that you don't want to talk about the war or is it you just don't want to talk with us about the war?" Charlotte stood at the sink, her back to Anne. "You cannot understand Anne. I know you lived through the war in America, but it was not the same. It was not fought on your doorstep. You did not live in fear that a Nazi might find the Resistance fighter that was hidden in the woods or the neighbor boy hidden in the cellar because he was old enough to be counted a man. At 13, old enough to be counted a man!" she spat. She turned to Anne then. "You want to hear of the war Anne? Do you want to hear of the many boys who did not come home or, if they did, came home like Jacques? Of the men who left countless orphans, of the whole family that was killed before our eyes because they had a tiny French flag on their door? Their son came home after the war to find his whole family massacred and killed himself. He survived the war, but what for when all he loved was dead? Is this what you want to hear Anne? Are these the things you are so anxious to have me tell you?" Anne lowered her eyes. "Forgive me, Charlotte, you are right. I had no business prying. You have been most hosptiable. I really should get back to the inn, as I have some things to do and I guess I just need some down time. I will see you at church tomorrow?" Charlotte took a deep breath. "Anne...." But Anne held up her hand. "No Charlotte, you are right. I have been terribly rude and I can only think it is because I am most tired. I need to rest this afternoon. I believe I am still jet lagged. Please don't feel you have done anything amiss. It is I. We will see each other at the picnic tomorrow and I thank you so much for today's hospitality." With that, she went to Charlotte, kissed her on both cheeks, smiled and went out the door. She was near tears. What was wrong with her, goading that poor woman to the edge like that? Was she trying to get closure for John so they could go home, because she did want to go home and they had only been there a week. She wanted to see her kids and grandkids and great grandkids. But she would hold on for John's sake. This was important to him and now he had a budding romance, no matter what Charlotte thought. And she wanted to find out about Jack also. What had happened to him? What did she expect when they came over here, that there would be a grave with his name on it? The Army and his buddies had already looked into that. She was going to go back to the inn and regroup. Like Scarlett O'Hara, she would think about it tomorrow.

John and Marie sat on the hill behind the small school, eating fruit and cheese and drinking wine. Always, the ever present wine. John was getting used to it and the French did not consider it an alcoholic drink. In fact, he hadn't seen anyone drink too much wine and become drunk. Since they drank it from a young age, moderation was always taught and it was mainly only taken with meals. Marie turned to him smiling. "So, how do you like our little village? See, I show it all to you in 2 hours flat, even the countryside! It is very small, but then I would not know how to live any other way." John looked out over the hillside at the farmhouses that dotted the countryside. "I too am from a fairly small town, only 6,000 people. That is considered a very small town in America. I like that I know all the faces on the streets and in the store. I understand how comfortable that is." He paused for a moment. He had felt exceptionally physically fit since he had been here and he hadn't been to a gym even once. Maybe it was all the walking or maybe he felt younger because of this lovely lady beside him. He didn't know. He just knew he didn't want it to end and felt better than he had in a long time. "Marie, tell me, could you ever think of living any other way? I mean, maybe in America with me?" Marie looked away from him. "I don't know, Jean. If we were younger, I would say we are lustful for each other and these feelings are only that, but it is strange, no, that we are both older and it is more than lust that I feel. We have both had opportunity and I have never felt this way in all those years and you say you have not." She paused for breath. "But to live away from Seaport Vue? I don't know. You don't even ask me just to move to Paris with you, but you ask me to leave my country. I don't know if I could do that. My children and grandchildren are here. And yours are in America. Maybe this will just have to be, how you say it, a fling?" John sighed. It seemed she was right. Wasn't that something? He finally found a woman he could be interested in and it was an impossible situation. He offered a quick prayer. "I know God means to prosper me and not harm me. You too, Marie, so let's leave this in His Hands. What do you say?" She smiled at him. "I think that is the best way. Perhaps we will think of something that will work for both of us. It is too bad we cannot be both in America and France at once." John looked at her elated. "Marie, I think you hit on it. I mean, I am not a poor man. Why couldn't we live half the year in Seaport Vue and the other half in Mt. Lilly? Why not?" Marie looked skeptical. "I don't know, John, that is a long time to be away from here and for you to be away from your people too." John took her hands. "But don't you see, Marie, you would be my people." She looked at him. "Nothing is impossible with God. Nothing. Let's leave it in His Hands, as you say. He will do the right thing." And for the first time since they had seen each other, they leaned in and found each other's lips.

When John and Marie returned to Charlotte's to pick up Anne, they found that she had returned to the inn. John was concerned, but Charlotte told him that she was just tired. "Please tell your mama, that I had a good time and I hope she will come again to my home. I will see her tomorrow at the picnic. Bonjour, Jean," and she turned and went into the kitchen. Marie followed her with puzzled eyes. "Something is wrong between our mothers, I can feel it. I wonder what could have happened. I will talk to my mama and you speak to yours and I will see you tomorrow. Let us go with our mothers and meet each other there, no? Then, you will meet my children and grandchildren, as they will be there too." They agreed and gave each other a quick kiss. It seemed something had gone wrong between the two moms, but considering both women, what could that be? He took the steps up to their room two at a time and pushed open the sitting room door. His mother looked up from the book she was reading and smiled. "Hello dear, did you have a good time with Marie?" She looked so benign that John had a hard time contemplating that she had a disagreement with Charlotte. "Yeah, Mom, it was great. How was your day?" He busied himself, taking his smartphone out of his pocket and his wallet and laying them on the table. "Oh, it was fine. I got a little tired and I came home." An uncomfortable silence ensued between them. "John", Anne said, hesitating. He looked up and saw his mother with her back to him, tracing the lines on the wallpaper. "Yes, Mom, is something wrong?" She turned to face him. "John", she repeated, "I don't think we should push these people to tell us about the war. Such bad memories they have, things they would rather not think about. I don't know how I would feel if people came and forced me to relive the day I got the telegram about your father over and over again. I am afraid I pushed Charlotte too far. She was terribly upset when I left her. We will see each other at the picnic tomorrow, but I am afraid I muffed it for a close friendship." She looked apologetically at her son. "And I know you like Marie and I want us all to be friends." John sat in the overstuffed chair. "I more than like her, Mom. We were talking today about a possible way to be together, perhaps 6 months in the states and 6 months in France. We are kind of leaving it up to God." Anne smiled and lifted her brow. "Kind of? You're going to take over if He can't handle it?" John laughed, his big laugh that sounded just like Jack's and Anne felt tears in her eyes. Even after all those years, she still had never heard anyone laugh like that but John and Jack. What a wonderful legacy, a laugh. "Good one, Mom, you got me. I guess He will do what He will, with or without my help. But I hope He realizes how much I love this woman." Anne said nothing, but wondered how he could love a woman that much in just two days. And then she thought back to when she had met his father. She knew immediately that it was love, just like John. She had liked Luke immensely and it had grown into a deep, sure love, but it was not like the fireworks and bells that she had with Jack. And John was no kid, nor was Marie. They must know a real attraction by now. But she did not know how it would work for them in their situation and in this day and age. She was glad she had lived in the time she had. Much of it was hard, but so much of it was good. The moral values, the family ties, the patriotism, Christ in the courts. People were proud to be Christians and love God and now, well just say it wasn't all that popular. Anne felt, well she felt just plain tired. So tired of all of this. She knew she would feel better after a little nap and then some supper tonight. She dreaded the picnic tomorrow since her set-to with Charlotte, but this too would pass. She knew that, at least, after 86 years of life. Soon she would be 87, only a month away. Where did the time go? "I'm going to lie down, dear. Wake me in time for supper, will you?" John looked at her carefully and then said, "Sure Mom." Anne went into her bedroom to lie down on the lovely bedspread and closed her eyes. She was looking into Luke's face. Jolene had just been born and she held her in her arms. Luke looked down at her tenderly. "Thank you darling," he whispered. "She's beautiful." She looked at the baby girl in her arms and looked again at Luke. When she had John, it had been her mother and father sitting on the side of her bed. Jack was not there. It was such a bittersweet moment. Jack's child, but no Jack. Tears ran down her face as she thought of Jack again. It was almost 6 years since she had gotten that telegram and, God help her, she still loved him. She loved Luke too, but not like she had loved Jack. Luke mistook her tears for happy tears and kissed her cheek. "We have a sweet little family now, don't we, a boy and a girl?" he had said. Then Bill had come along and Luke said he thought their family was big enough. She and Jack had decided they wanted at least 6 kids (they figured they could each handle 3 alone) and had enjoyed the planning and the doing. Luke, as much as he did like children and they liked him, wanted no more children and at age 27, Anne was done having children. She and Luke had been happy, but she had often wondered what her life would have been like if Jack had lived. Then she saw him. Her Jack, smiling down at her, laughing his laugh, just as handsome as she remembered. His eyes flashing. What was he saying? He was saying something to her. "Annie, I am right here, right here." She reached out for him, but he faded into the dark and she woke up in a cold sweat. Opening her eyes, she felt herself breathing shallowly, short quick breaths and tried to slow them down. The light in her room switched on and John stood there looking scared. "Mom, are you alright? I thought you called out for me." Anne tried to collect herself and smile at her son. "I had a dream, son. I thought I saw your father. I'm okay now." And as if to prove it, she sat up on the side of her bed and stood up. "Well, I was just about ready to wake you anyhow, Mom, because it's 5:15 pm and you know how Madame Cheveneaux is about us being late for supper!" "Oh dear, did I sleep 2 1/2 hours? I will never get to sleep tonight!" And with that she hurried to tidy her hair and clothes so they could go to supper. Madame Cheveneaux served them and then sat down herself at the supper table. Anne suspected she enjoyed the company. Tonight she was excited about all the things she would make for the picnic tomorrow, her famous croissants, her succulent salad, her dreamy desserts. "Madame, I am sure your table will be empty before anyone else's! Why even Father said your croissants were the best in town," John exclaimed and Marie Fern Cheveneaux beamed at the compliment from her spirtual leader. She adored Father Jacques and thought him the closest thing to God one could be. "What should we bring?" Anne asked. Madame Cheveneaux waved her hand in dismissal. "Don't worry, my dear. For a small fee, I can make you the most wonderful appetizers. They have cheese and ham and garlic and you just bake them for a tiny bit and voila! They are tres bein!" She kissed her fingers and looked at them expectantly. If anyone could make her laugh, it was Madame Cheveneaux, but she did not know it. She was being perfectly serious. "By all means, Madame, I would be so honored to pay a small fee for such a wonderful appetizer. Shall I pick it up when I go?" Anne asked innocently. "Oh, yes, that would be best. People will think you are the best cook, Madame Crawford. I will not say a word and you don't either!" Madame Cheveneaux gave her a conspiratoral wink and Anne winked back to keep from laughing. Of course, people would know Marie Fern Cheveneaux made that appetizer and Marie Fern would pretend she hadn't and then she would tell that person in confidence that the poor American lady did not want to go empty handed, so what could she do? And then she would intimate she did it out of the goodness of her heart. Anne smiled. Some people needed to have their attention that way, because that was the only attention they got. She could not begrudge poor Marie Fern Cheveneaux her 15 minutes of fame. "John dear, please pay Madame Cheveneaux for her services as a chef will you? I will see you up in the room." And with that Anne gave a little wave and went up the stairs.

The weather was fine for the picnic the next day and by 8:45 am, John and Anne were on their way to 9:00 am mass. Madame Cheveneaux had already attended the 6:30 am mass. She had knocked on their door at 6:00 am in a flurry, stating she must fly ("she actually said "must fly!") She told them she had left their dish on the counter downstairs. It was a 10 minute walk to the church and by 8:45 am, they were on their way, Madame Cheveneaux's dish in hand. As they neared the church, they heard voices coming from within. They walked into a group of about 75 people, laughing, talking and trading babies. As Father Jacques made his way up to the altar, everyone took their seats and the murmuring grew quiet. Anne found the mass interesting, but she couldn't follow it because it was all in French. He must have been a good speaker though because he held everyone's attention, John's included. After communion, in which Anne and John partook being believers, Father gave the benediction and everyone made movements to leave. They filed out of the door and headed for the back of the church. John and Anne stayed seated until everyone had left. The looked at each other, shrugged and followed the crowd out the back door into the back yard of the church where the party was already in full swing. A group of older men were throwing silver balls at smaller colored balls. Anne wasn't sure of the object of the game, but it was interesting to watch. "Ah, Anne, Jean welcome, welcome!" they heard Father Jacques' voice across the yard. He was making his way through to them in record time. "I am so glad you could could come! I was just telling Marie that you were at 9:00 am mass. I am sorry; I forgot you are not fluent in French, however, I hope you felt the presence of the Lord there. I see you were watching the men play petanque. It is a fun game and, if I was not the host, I would join them, but right now let's go find Marie and Charlotte. They should be right over there." Father made a beeline for a large tree and Anne and John could do nothing but follow him. Anne slowed a little as she noticed Marie and Charlotte within a group of people. Marie immediately freed herself and came over to them. "I am so glad you came. Mama and I have been waiting for you." She addressed this to Anne, who smiled weakly. Charlotte came out from behind a sea of women and approached Anne. She took Anne's hands in hers and said softly, "I am so glad you came. I am sorry about yesterday. Can we start again?" Anne smiled. "My fault entirely and of course. I am so glad you want to." Charlotte hugged her. "Of course I want to. I must introduce you to some ladies. This is Katherine, Michaela, Suzanne and Kimberly. These are my closest friends. And Suzette, Linda, Joyce and Margueritte of course also. My sisters. My brother, Eugene, is around somewhere, probably with the men playing petanque, but you can meet him later." The ladies nodded and smiled and then Charlotte waved to them and said she would see them later. Marie and John had already wandered off together and Charlotte took Anne's arm and strolled toward the tables. "Let's get rid of that," she said, referring to the covered dish that Anne still held in her hands. Charlotte took the dish from Anne's hands when they reached the table. "Let me guess, Marie Fern made that and told you to tell everyone you made it and now she is tsk, tsking to everyone and calling you a poor dear, am I right?" Anne laughed at the accurate description. "But she is a nice woman underneath it all, I think," Anne said. "I just think she needs the money, but more, she needs the attention." "Quite right, Anne. You are very, how you say, sensitive to such things. Ah, here is my grandson, Andre Richard, named for his great grandfathers. Andre!" she called, waving her hand to a handsome young man in his early 40's. He looked familiar to Anne, like any young American. John really favored his French heritage. You could see the coloring and the "French look" in this young man as she had seen it in John at that age. "Grandmere!" he greeted Charlotte, kissing her on both cheeks. He straightened and smiled down at Anne. "You must be the mother of the man that my mother speaks of incessantly. I need to meet him before I become so sick of him that I make an unfair judgment of him!" His eyes twinkled and Anne knew he was just teasing and so she laughed. "Oh, there are Marie and John now," she said, catching sight of Marie's eye. Marie smiled when she saw Andre Richard standing with them. She pulled John over to their little circle. "Jean, I would like you to meet my son, Andre Richard. I have spoken of you often and he has demanded a meeting!" she laughed. Andre Richard and John laughed too, but Anne could see the two men

63

sizing each other up. Andre Richard extended his hand. "Jean, a friend of my mother's is a friend of mine, but even more importantly, Father Jacques speaks highly of you, so I guess you are good to know!" They all laughed. Anne noticed that the older French people spoke better English than the younger ones. That was interesting. "Mama, guess who is here? The old medecin, Monsieur Colbert. How old is he now, 102?" They spoke in French and then Charlotte translated. "He is old and senile. He was a great man in his day, saved many people, hid many people. He even hid one man in a grave and then dug him up after the Nazis were gone. He always felt he didn't do enough, but he did much more than many. Poor man. His great mind is gone." "Let's go see him, Grandmere. Everyone should have the privilege of meeting the medecin. I have not seen him for a long time. He lives in the hospital and we all take care of him." Charlotte explained more as they walked toward where the doctor was holding court. "We have a home where the old can go for care. It is run by two single sisters and all of us take turns going into help. At the moment they have 5 people, but the doctor has been there almost 10 years. He was quite spry up into his 90s." They had reached the doctor and he looked up as they approached. "Why are you up young man? You should be in bed." He addressed himself to Andre Richard, who smiled indulgently. "I am much better now, medecin, and can be up and about," he answered, humoring him. "Not with those wounds, not yet, not yet. Stay hidden boy, stay hidden." He started to talk to himself and some of the men started patting his shoulder and reassuring him that all was well. "Sometimes he reverts back to the war," Marie explained. "He was so important. I just don't think he has ever let go of it. Poor man, he deserved better." "Oh, I don't know," John interjected. "I think he has it pretty good, in a town where everyone loves and cares for him, 102 years old. A lot of people have it a lot worse. He seems happy to me." He smiled and Marie intertwined her arm with his. "I think you are correct," she said. "We are all very fortunate." If Anne did not miss the look that passed between Marie and John, she knew Charlotte and Andre Richard did not miss it either. They started to walk away and heard the doctor call, "My boy, it is too soon, too soon. Stay hidden. Heed me." Anne turned back to look and the doctor was looking directly at Andre Richard, who shrugged and smiled and continued walking. "Ah there is my errant family now. Emile! Julie! Come and meet some people," he called in French to a young couple that looked to be in their very early 20s. They came over and Andre Richard introduced them as his daughter and son-in-law. Greetings and translations were exchanged and small talk made. The young couple soon saw some friends, made their apologies and walked away from the little group. "Ladies and Gentleman," a voice called in French. Anne knew it was Father Jacques before she turned around. He stood on a small incline in the yard a wineglass in hand. "I know you are all wondering about the Americans. Please introduce yourselves to Anne and her son John Crawford. They speak a little French!" he said and everyone laughed. John was checking out the smartphone and smiled when he realized what Father Jacques said. "I propose a toast to a great doctor, a great man, a great hero and a great citizen of France, our own Doctor Colbert." And he held his glass high and toasted the elderly doctor who sat in his chair talking to himself, cautioning men of the past to keep themselves hidden.

Anne was done in for the night, so at 5:30 pm, John and Marie walked her back to Madame Chevereau's. They said their goodnights and then decided to stroll around town and perhaps go by the pub and have something to drink. Many friends greeted them as they entered the pub, many who John had met that day at the picnic. He liked Seaport Vue and he liked the people and he especially liked being one half of a couple again. How wonderful to have a captivating woman on your arm, to have your heart beating quickly once again when you catch her eye. He felt like he had when he and Cathy had been new and he liked it. He liked it very much. A few of the men were cold to him, but John chalked that up to sour grapes. He imagined many men had been trying to win the beautiful widow for many years and had been unsuccessful and then suddenly a rich doctor (yes, John had overheard a couple of men calling him that, if they only knew!) comes from America and dazzles her with promises. Well, he could assure them, he was the one who was dazzled. He was going to have a very hard time leaving her, but he didn't know how he could leave his kids and grandkids and Mom. That would be too hard. He couldn't bear to be over here when Mom went and he knew she couldn't live forever. But she could live for another 10 or 15 years and then what? Well, he wasn't going to think about that tonight. He was going to enjoy having his first real date in years. He saw Father Jacques and waved. Did that man never tire? He had been at the picnic all day, heard confessions all Saturday and had served Mass this morning twice. He had to be as old or older than Mom. John shook his head and smiled. He should be so energetic. Marie took his hand and he smiled at her. "Jean, there is a man here, a friend of my uncle. He was a boy in the war, about 8, but he seems to remember some things. He heard you were looking for your father and he thinks he might be able to help." She pulled him in the direction of a man who sat at a back table by himself. He was waiting for his turn to play pool. "I will have to translate because Louis does not speak hardly any English at all, this is good?" Marie asked. "Yes, of course, that will be fine. For some reason, I didn't expect to see a pool table here," John answered. Marie laughed. "That was sent by some soldiers that came here after the war. They think we need to keep our young men busy and out of trouble, so they give us pool. Mama has an American record with the song, "Pool with a capital P and that says with T and that is Pool!" She sang it a little and John was pretty sure she was talking about one of the songs from the soundtrack of the Music Man. He laughed with her and quipped, "And she sings too!" The other man stood up. "Manifique, Marie!" he beamed at her

66

and kissed her on both cheeks. "Bonjour, Monsieur. Je suis, Louis." John shook the older man's hand. "Bonjour, Louis. Je suis Jean." The niceties out of the way, Louis started to tell his story in rapid fire French and even Marie had to slow him down so she could translate. "When I was a young boy," she translated, "I saw a light in the sky. It looked like a fire coming down. I ran toward the woods where it hit, but there were some men coming too, so I hid behind a tree. Lots of men come from the village, Seaport Vue, even my pere. They look and try to put out fire, but it still burn. I stay for about an hour. I see them carrying something, but I don't know what. The next day I ask my pere about the fire flying from the sky and what did they carry out from the woods. He just look at me and say, "Louis, you had bad dream. This never happened. Do you hear what I say? This never happened." So, I am a boy, he is my pere. It never happened. I knew secrets were important. I knew people died when you didn't keep secrets, so I always kept it. But now, I guess it doesn't matter." Marie finished translating and Louie looked up at him, curious. "Cela vous aide pas?" Louis asked. John knew he had just asked him if that would help. "I don't know, maybe, merci." he answered Louis and Marie translated for him. He nodded, shook John's hand and then it was his turn for pool. Marie and John moved into a vacant table. "How do you say, pennies for thoughts?" Marie asked lightly. John smiled. "Well, I was thinking it's an interesting story, but I don't know if it means anything. I mean, who else is alive that witnessed that scene? Father Jacques was being held captive, the doctor can't remember his own name, your father is away. Is there anyone else in town that might know of that night?" Marie thought. "Not that I know of. Old Monsieur Beaulieu cannot speak of the war and I am not sure he was even here at that time." "I already spoke with him," John said. "Dead end." Marie scrunched up her mouth in thought. "Oh, I know. There is a veteran's meeting once a month for the old veterans and the younger veterans at Ciel D'azur, a town about 15 miles away. Pere always goes, but this time he will miss it. It is being held on next Tuesday. If you like, I will take you or we can go in your car. All the men in the surrounding towns will be there. Will that be helpful?" John beamed at her. "Marie, I could just kiss you! Yes, that would help!" Marie gave him a saucy look. "Well, we can leave here and go for a walk and then you certainly can kiss me!" He raised his eyebrows and gave an imitation of a suave smile. "Oui, oui, madam, I am at your service. Lead the way." And John followed the lovely lady out of the pub.

First thing in the morning, after another five star breakfast served by Madame Chevereau, John and Anne jumped into the Renault and headed out toward another little town 15 miles away. The weather was absolutely beautiful and it promised to be the same all day. Driving along with the windows down, they started to sing "Frere Jacques" and sang and laughed loudly. When they would stumble over the words, they would make them up, causing Anne to remember all the fun she had with John when he was a little boy. "The only words that I am really sure of are Din, Din, Don," she said laughing. "I taught this to you when you were young, because your father was French and Jacques was in the title." She smiled at him and he looked at her quizzedly. "Did you love Dad when you married him? I mean Dad Luke," he clarified himself. Anne thought back 60 some odd years ago.

Anne was wined and dined and loved. Luke had been almost through law school when he went to war and finished when he returned. He passed the Bar on his first try. He and Anne were married the day after he passed the Bar. She had been unsure, but now that she knew Jack was dead, this seemed the best thing to do. He was a good, upstanding and very handsome man. He was kind, fun, smart and most of all, he was an excellent father to John and, oh how John needed a father. The little boy thought Luke was the best thing since sliced bread and Luke did nothing to dispel that notion. He took John with him almost everywhere he went, he bragged on him to everyone (thus endearing him to her heart) and played and talked and laughed with him. He taught him and disciplined him gently. Did she love him? She didn't know because the feelings she had for this brilliant, kind and handsome man were so different from the ones she had for Jack. Where Luke was gentle and sweet in their lovemaking, Jack had been eager and fiery. When Jack had been reckless, Luke was careful. Yes, she loved him, but differently than she had loved Jack, because he wasn't her first lover or her first husband. But he was John's first father and he had loved him dearly. He loved being John Crawford, Luke Crawford's son, because everyone thought so highly of his father. He was a war hero, a decent and just man, a pillar of society. He was the Dad that all the kids liked, the one that would defend someone who had no money to pay him, the champion of the underdog. Luke was wonderful, but did she love him when she married him?

May 25, 1944 Luke

He had told that kid that if anything happened to him, he would see to it that his wife was cared for. When he got the kid's address from the chaplin, he was surprised to see it was his hometown. He'd never seen or heard of the kid before and it was a small town where everyone knew everyone else, so he could only think he had moved there after Luke had started law school. He hadn't been home much after college. When his college sweetheart eloped with his good friend, he had kind of given up on women. That was the main reason he had enlisted in the Army. He supposed he had studied too hard and too much for a party girl like Peggy. She wanted to go out all the time and he just didn't have the time or money. His so called friend, however, wasn't as serious about school and he did have the money and made the time. Oh, well, his heart hadn't really been broken when Peggy left him. He sat on a park bench under a tree in his dress uniform, watching a young woman push her child on a swing, at least he assumed it was her child as he called her Mommy. Something about this girl, because she wasn't much more than that, looked familiar to him. He stood and walked closer for a better look. Who was that? He knew her. The girl looked at him a little warily and then laughed at something the child said. No, it couldn't be! Was that Anne Morgan, Ron's cousin? She was just a kid last time he had seen her, 10, maybe 11 years old. . She looked his way again, not sure if she should grab her child and run. He probably did look a little threatening, coming closer and staring at her. Better to ask and find out. "Anne, Anne is that you?" he asked. She had been startled and then looked at him closely, breaking into a beautiful slow grin. "Luke, Luke Crawford!" she has answered and the rest was history. Her little boy wanted a push and Luke complied. It felt so good doing normal things with normal people. Pushing a child on a swing, for instance. And then Anne had told him her last name. He couldn't believe it. He had come here to tell Jack's widow he had known him, to give her some information, but he couldn't just yet. He was captivated the moment he spoke to her. He started a courtship and this time nothing interfered with winning the woman he loved. He fully intended to tell her he had been Jack's C.O., but the time was never right and she was so fragile. And the boy! What a character. It didn't take Luke long to fall in love with that little guy, not when bright brown eyes were staring up at him like he was the best thing since sliced bread, not when he dogged his every footstep like he was his hero. But Luke never forgot Jack. He called Jack's closest buddies in the unit to have them comb the area where Jack should have gone down for any clues as to his fate. These were some of his best men and they had a personal interest in finding Jack. They came up with nothing. Luke had waited until he knew for sure there was no hope of finding Jack before he proposed to Anne. He could feel that Anne still had strong feelings for Jack and he knew she was marrying him mostly out of lonliness and to give John a father. But he didn't care. He loved them both and he had promised Jack LaFontaine that if anything happened to him he would make sure his wife was cared for. And, unbeknownest to Jack, he would also take care of his son with a father's love that he was sure Jack would have given John if he had lived. He had put that young pilot in harm's way as his C.O. and it seared his conscious. Every time he lost a boy on a mission, because that's all most of them really were, boys, he was on his knees, torn with pain. He knew it was his job, but it took a bit of him every time one of his boys went down. He did everything he could to find out the fate of his men and retrieve their bodies and he had found them all, save Jack LaFontaine. He hoped his death had been painless.

"Yes, I must have loved him or I would not have married him. It was different than it was with Jack, but thinking of spending my life without Luke was not an option, so your answer is yes, yes, I loved him very much, even more than I knew at the time." Her reward was the brilliant smile that had been Jack's that John flashed at her. "I'm glad, Mom. I am glad you got to have two great loves in your life," John said. They both seemed content with her answer and continued on their journey to find out more about the "first great love" of Anne's life. They took time to stop by the side of the road so Anne could gather some beautiful wildflowers. She wasn't sure what they were, but she picked them anyway, laying them between her and John in the front seat. John eyed them and quipped, "Sure hope that isn't some French version of poison oak!" Anne chuckled. They passed over a small hill and came onto what seemed to be outlying farms of a village that could be seen in the distance. John marveled at how he could see for a couple of miles out without obstruction and they sped toward the town in the distance. The sign read, "Cristalline de la mer" or Crystal of the Sea. That bode well and since the sun was shining on the outlying water, their spirts were high. Pulling into the quaint little town (it seems like all the towns that they had visited were quaint), they looked for a place to park. One thing that Anne and John had noticed about the towns that they had been in is that there were not many cars. A lot of people rode bicycles or motorcycles or walked. Some people had a mule. They pulled in front of what looked like a general store and decided to go in and look around and see if maybe this town had a library. It did not look promising, but they decided to ask anyway. Inside the store, they found a young woman waiting on an older couple. They looked around until she was free. "Oui, puis je vou aider?", she asked. "Yes, thank you, could you tell us if there is a libraray in this town?" She thought for a moment. "Non, pas ici, mais dans Jolieville." They looked at each other. "The only one is in Jolieville and we have been there, right?" Anne asked. "Oui," he answered his mother. "Thank you," he addressed the young woman. "I mean, merci". Anne smiled and they started out, to be almost toppled over by a small boy racing into the store. John caught Anne as she stumbled. "Francis! Vilain garcon! Viens ici tout de suite!" (Francis! You naughty boy! Come here at once!)the young woman at the counter cried out, racing around from behind the counter to Anne. She grabbed the little boy's arm. "Presenter des excuses a cette dame a la fois!" (Apologize to this lady at once!), she demanded. The little boy hung his head and said in a barely audible voice. "Je suis desole, Madame, ne vous facez pas." (I am sorry, Madame. Don't be angry). Anne was a little shaken, but she also loved children. She placed her hand on the child's head. "It's alright little one. You just have too much outdoors in you for the indoors." The boy did not understand the words, but he did understand the kindness in the words and the smile on the face of this gracious madam. Unhooking a medal from his shirt, he handed it to Anne. "Ici,

Madame, vous pouvez avoir ma medaille. Il est mon meilleur tresor!" (Here Madam, you may have my medal. It is my best treasure!) Anne took the small wing shaped medal from the boy's hand. She looked at John. "It's an American wings medal that pilots wore. Jack had one." John took the medal and studied it. It was definitely old. After consulting his smartphone, he asked the boy, in French, where he had gotten the medal. "My grandfather gave it to me," he replied in French. "His father gave it to him! It is very, very old, non?" The boy beamed with pride and John forced a smile. "Very old, oui," he replied. "But I cannot take this without giving something in return. What would you like?" The boy's eyes widened. "Anything?" he asked. "Well, within reason," John replied, knowing the minds of small boys. "I would like a bicycle!" the boy said happily. "Francis, non c'est trop!" (Francis, no, that is too much!) But John smiled at the boy and his mother and replied in French, "No, it is fine. Show me the bicycle you want or if you would like, I will give you the money." Francis' mother was clearly embarrased. She bade Francis go with John and Anne, apparently to show them where the bicycle was. He led them to a small garage a few blocks away. Outside stood a refurbished bicycle painted blue with a basket on the handlebars. John looked at the small boy and then at the bicycle. "Are you sure you can ride that?" he asked. The boy nodded his head vigorously and ran up to the bike as a man in coveralls came out of the garage wiping his hands on a rag. John quickly explained to him in French that he wanted to purchase the bicycle. The man named a price of $25, which Anne thought the man thought he would probably never get, and John paid him in Euros. "Merci, monsieur." the mechanic said and patted Francis' head as went back into the garage. The boy beamed at John and Anne realized the money was worth that look on the child's face. He instantly got on the bike and rode like an expert, calling something over his shoulder as he sped away. "I missed that," Anne said, "what did he say?" John chuckled. "He said, thank you rich American man, I must show

73

my mother and my grandfather to show I got the best deal or close to that." Anne laughed and shook her head and then asked John for the medal. He handed it to her. She inspected the medal for a time and then handed it back to John. "It's just like Jack's. It's an old WW II pilot's wings, American." He looked at his mother. "Could it be, Mom? I mean, could it be that these are Jack's? Or could they be another American pilot? I wonder where the guy got these? Did he find them? Were they given to him? Maybe we should talk to the grandfather." Anne sighed. "Well, I suppose we could. This is the first real lead we have had. Alright, let's go back to the store and see what we can find." And with that, they returned to the general store to speak with Francis' mother. As it turned out, her father was working on repairs in the back of the store, however, her grandfather who had originally had the medal, was no longer living. They stepped into the back of the store to find a man approximately the age of John repairing an old toaster. He actually had a repair shop in the back of the store. He looked up as they came in. He said nothing, but returned to his work, ignoring them. John cleared his throat. "Excuse us, Sir," he started in French. "We would like to make an inquiry as to where your father obtained these wings." He held out his hand in which the wings sat and the man looked at them. He gave John a nondescript look and then resumed his work. Since it did not look like he was going to speak to them, John tried again. "My father was a flier for the U.S. Army Airforce in WW II and he was supposed to have crashed somewhere near this area. We are just trying to find information on him." The man continued to work, so John and Anne turned to leave. "My father gave that to me when I was a boy," he answered in passable English. "His friend gave it to him so they would always be dearest friends. He said it was his best treasure. So it was mine, so it was Francis'. Why did he give it to you?" he asked. "Did you hear the noise in the store? He ran into my mother and wanted to make it up. He's a sweet little guy. I don't want to take something that is important to him. Here, why don't you give it back to him?" John offered. The man looked up at him. "If it is your father's it is more important you have it. Besides, he has a bicycle," the Frenchman said, smiling a small smile. John chuckled. So he had heard the whole thing. "I know this. My father's friend lived in another town. The boy came to visit his aunt and uncle in the summer and he and my father became close friends. This was given as a boys' pact, you know how it is with young boys." John started. "Which town was he from, do you know?" Francis' grandfather shrugged. "Non, just one of the other small towns from around here. Papa never said where. Sorry, that is all I know." He picked up the toaster to resume his work. "Here give this to Francis. I don't want to take it from him." The man smiled. "Non, you keep it. It is important you have it. I wish you God's blessings on your search." He smiled and looked down at his work and they got the message that he really wanted to get back to it." One more thing, Monsieur," John asked. "What is your name?" "I am Cecil DuPont, as was my father." John smiled and held out his hand. Cecil shook it. "Au revoir, then Monsieur, we will detain you no longer. Merci." John and Anne left the store, waving at Francis' mother as they left. They walked in silence out to the Renault. John held the door for his mother and then got in himself and started the engine. "Well, we have a few pieces of the puzzle," Anne said. "Yes, John replied, "now if they would just start falling in place." The trip back to Seaport Vue was quiet, each lost in his and her own thoughts. As they pulled into the tiny village, Ann saw a man walking unsteadily down the street. At first she thought the man was drunk, but when she looked again, she realized it was Dr. Colbert. "John, stop the car!" she said urgently and jumped out as soon as he had stopped. She rushed up to the old man and took his hand. "Doctor, are you alright? Would you like us to take you back to your home?" John was there by that time and gave her a look that said they should just take him back and not converse about it. "Non, non I must find him. He must stay hidden. It is too early. He is too fragile." John put his hand on the old doctor's shoulder. "Why is it too early, doctor?" he asked. Anne was amazed at how good John's French had become. She could make out some of the words, but not speak as well as John. "He is not well yet. He is still fragile in his mind. Don't you see?" He turned to John and pleaded. "Please Richard, help me find him." The old man looked confused and pulled at John's coat. "Jacques? But you are old. Where is he, where is he? Help me to find him." The old man collapsed weeping in John's arms just as Father Jacques some other people who had obviously been searching for him came into view. "Doctor! Is he alright?" Father asked John, kneeling down to check on the old man. "He needs to go to bed. He is exhausted. He was looking for someone, a man he said should stay hidden, the same one he was looking for the day of the picnic," John said. Father nodded. "Yes, all the young men he worried about. So many had a rough time, as I told you. The doctor watched out for them. He must think he is still in the war." John and Father Jacques were able to get the doctor into the Renault and drive the few blocks to the makeshift nursing home, run by the two sisters. Anne rode along with them while the rest of the searchers followed on foot. They took Dr. Colbert into the home and up to his room where the ministrations were taken over by several capable older ladies. "Merci, monsieur," they smiled him. Many patted John on the back and gave Anne a hug. They had aided their beloved doctor and they had gone up a notch in the town's estimation. After declining coffee and the ever present pastries, pleading fatigue they made their way to Madame Chevereaux's. To their surprise, the spry little Frenchwoman had whipped up a souffle and had a table set for them. "My treat!" she beamed. "You saved the doctor. You are heroes!" Although they protested they were not heroes, she insisted they eat for free and chattered on about the doctor, giving them all the details of his past. "Of course, I was just a young girl in the war, but we all knew the doctor was a great man, him and Father Pierre, whom the

Nazis killed." She teared up for a few seconds and cleared her throat. "He was a great man." She smiled at them again and continued, "Dr. Colbert was all business. He didn't play with us children as Father did, but he had a strength and everyone of us knew that he would take care of us when we were hurt and he did. He was a very gentle man, but he also was a strong and brave one. When Jacques was hurt he treated his burns without him going to a hospital. I suppose, looking back on it, that was quite a feat without a hospital, but there was no other choice." John looked up. "How was he burned?" Madame Chevereaux frowned. "I don't recall." "Then there were many man who were brought here for treatment. Dr. Colbert was the only doctor for miles around. The ones who could be moved were brought here, but Dr. Colbert went to many surrounding towns too. He overworked himself terribly, but still he kept on. John moved his food around on his plate. "Yes, but the ones he brought here, they all went home after the war, didn't they?" "Yes, most of them. But some didn't have a place to go and stayed. Rene was one of those, I guess. He was staying with the Dumeres and then he married Charlotte." Anne didn't say anything. She had heard all of this from Charlotte already. "Thank you Madame Devereaux. I hope you won't take offense if we go on up to our rooms. We are pretty tired," Anne stated. "Oh, oui, madame, monsiuer please go and rest. I will see you in the morning for breakfast, non?" "Oui," John answered and followed his mother upstairs.

Anne and John were just finishing breakfast when Charlotte and Marie Louise came into the dining room. "Bonjour, Anne and Jean!" Charlotte called gaily. "I hope you do not have plans today because this is the day we will take you to the big veterans' meeting in Ciel D'azur!" Noting John and Anne's stunned looks, Marie Louise explained. "We forgot all about this until early this morning. Mama and I met each other halfway to each other's house. We knew you would want to go and it only happens once a month." She paused for breath. "Can you go?" she asked. "Of course we can go!" Anne replied. This is what we came for!" John hurriedly downed the rest of his coffee and they all piled into the small Renault. "I think we have gotten more good out of this rental car than we do out of the ones we actually own," John joked. "Which way?" Within an hour they were in the lovely little town whose name meant in English "Blue Skies". Anne could not get enough of these lovely little villages. She was afraid she was going to be very disappointed when she finally explored Paris. The meeting was not until 10:00 am, so they had some time to spare. Marie Louise and Charlotte were fairly familiar with the town, as they had friends here. They suggested they stop and see if their friends were home, so John drove slowly up the street that the ladies had named. "I will see if they are home," Charlotte said, jumping out of the car and walking up to a pretty little house with a brightly colored door. "Marie Louise, why do people have brightly colored doors?" Anne asked the younger woman. Marie Louise looked perplexed for a moment and then shrugged her shoulders. "Why not?" Anne chuckled to herself. Why not, indeed? A door says a lot about it's occupants. Charlotte came back to the car. "They are home, but are just getting ready to go someplace. They want to know if we can come back when the meeting is over. They may have some information for you." John cast a sideways glance at Charlotte. "What kind of information?" he queried. "Oh, I don't know, but her father was in the war and she may have some of her own stories. You can never tell what they may lead to." They started on toward the village square under Charlotte's direction. "Always there is a center of town where everyone gathers," she explained. "Perhaps I will see some friends whom we can talk with. On meeting day, everyone is always in town from all the other places within 20 miles. It's a very lively place once a month!" She looked eagerly out the window, craning her neck to see who was there. "Take it easy, Mama, we will park in just a minute and then you may look all you want!" Marie Louise laughed. John parked the car in a vacant side road. "It really is crowded," he remarked. "It looks like a festival or something!" Marie Louise laughed, hugging his arm. "In a way it is. The people bring goods to sell and it has a very festive air about it." Anne stepped out of the car. relishing the beautiful day and the carnival atomosphere. Seeing all the children with candy on a stick and laughing brought tears to her eyes. "I miss my grandchildren and greats", she thought to herself. "I want to go home". But they were still far from finding any trace of Jack and she did not want to be the reason they went home early. "Oh, Jean, Anne, look! The veterans are going to have their meeting in a room at the town hall. See the sign?" Anne looked at the sign to which Charlotte pointed and thought she might be able to understand the the word, veteran. Charlotte laughed at her own faux pas. "I am sorry. I keep forgetting you are not French!". She looked at her a little sadly and a tear came to her eye. Quickly she turned away and started talking excitedly. "Oh, look at that time! We have only 20 minutes until it starts. Let's get something to drink and then go on in." They fought their way to a booth that sold soft drinks and, of course, wine. Charlotte and Marie Louise purchased a glass of wine, but Anne and John went with a good old American lemonade. It tasted a little different and then Anne realized they had put other fruit in it also. It actually was very good. The four friends strolled leisurely over to the town hall and climbed the steps up to the room where the meeting would be held. "There's always stairs aren't there?" Anne remarked and Charlotte smiled at her with empathy. Finally, they walked into the room 5 minutes before the meeting and took their seats. There was at least 50 people there. Anne was surprised. She thought it was going to be 10 or 12 old men around a table, but there were younger men that had served in Korea all the way up to the ones who had just returned from Afghanistan. Anne knew she was rusty on her world history when Marie Louise pointed out a friend of her's that had served in Bosnia and a hometown boy that had served in the Gulf. Shortly, the meeting was called to order. There were a few spectators besides them, but not many. It was a replay of the mass for Anne. It was all in French and she only caught a few words, but she did realize that her French was actually getting better. When the meeting broke up, Marie Louise pulled John over to the hometown boy to introduce him, but Charlotte took Anne's arm and guided her to an elderly man. The gentleman was stooped and wrinkled and surely had seen better days, but his smile was bright and his eyes were clear. "Maybe because he has lenses like me and doesn't have to wear glasses," Anne thought. "Anne, may I present Monsieur Buzzard, the oldest member of the veterans' gatherings. Rene is the second oldest." Anne smiled and shook the man's hand. Charlotte switched to French and made the introduction to the old Frenchman. She continued to speak and Anne thought she must be explaining her situation. When Charlotte finished speaking, Monsieur Buzzard turned to her, bowed from the waist and spoke in halting English. "Madame, I may help you or I may not. I know one thing about an American flier who crashed. He did not live, but he was buried in an unmarked grave by the townspeople. They could not take the chance of marking it because of the Nazis and they did not want it desecrated." "Where?" Anne queried excitedly, "where is he buried?" The old man shrugged. "That is the problem, Madame. The grave was unmarked and over the years, it has hidden itself. Perhaps, though, there are some in town that know more than I about this, non?" He bowed once again, smiled and excused himself. Anne was a little disappointed and Charlotte took her arm. "Well, do not be too sad, mi ami. My friend, Cheri may still know something that may help you." They walked towards Marie Louise and John. "Why don't we go down and get lunch and then go see if Cheri and Thomas are home? Is anyone as hungry as I am?" Charlotte asked gaily. The four of them went back down into the festival atmosphere and pushed their way through the happy crowds. Anne could feel herself fading a bit, but did not want to put a damper on the excitement of their little group. She held tightly to Charlotte's arm as they made their way through the crowd. Finally, they sat at a vacant table that Marie Louise had spotted and ran like a kid to save. She was laughing and so was John as he caught up with her and sat in the seat next to her. "Quick Mamas, someone may take your chairs if you are not quick!" Marie Louise smiled. John and Marie Louise looked at each other so intently that Anne was almost embarrased. How were these two going to reconcile ever leaving each other? Charlotte and Marie Louise decided to go to the stand and order for everyone, since they knew which food was the best. That left John and Anne at the table together. John touched his mother's hand. "You okay, Mom? You look a little bit peaked. Are you going to be able to make it through the afternoon?" Anne smiled and looked into the face of her beloved son. "Oh, John, when you get my age, you do get tired and I have been more tired lately than usual, but I am fine with rest. It feels good to sit here and then after we eat we will see Charlotte's friends and then maybe we will find something out or, at the rate we are going, maybe not. But anyhow, I am fine. I really am. I want answers as much as you do and I want to stay until we get them." John sighed. "I wonder if I am chasing a dream, Mom. If anyone fits the bill as my father, it is Father Jacques. Does he seem at all familiar to you?" John looked so eager that Anne just wanted to acquiese and say it was him. But she knew in her heart that Father Jacques was not her Jack. "I don't think so, John. I really don't think your father survived. I think he could be that unknown flier or he could have gone down in the water or he could have just crashed and burned. I don't hold out much hope for actually finding out what happened to him, but at least we have an idea that it could have been him that went down around here. We might just have to be satisfied with that." John looked at her. "And you are not sure about Claude?" Anne shook her head. "Perhaps, but I always thought I would know in my heart if I saw him again and I did not feel that for Claude. I only felt compassion." IJohn sighed. "I just didn't want to go home until I found something, Mom, but you are fading before my eyes and I need to get you home to your family. And, truth be told, much as I hate to leave Marie Louise, I miss my family too." He smiled wryly at her. "Here we are finally!" Charlotte trilled. "The line was not as long as it seemed and it went faster than we thought." They deposited the food on the table unwrapping croissants and meat and cheese and dishes that neither John nor Anne were familiar. They also had brought some devilish looking desserts. "Wow, this looks great!" John stated and they all dug in and started eating. Laughing, talking and eating, Anne felt a sense of peace and friendship. Even if they never found what they were looking for, they had found some people who would always mean a lot ot them, maybe even more than that. She still didn't know what would go on between John and Marie Louise. "Well", Charlotte stated standing up. "Shall we go on to Cheri's?" They all agreed and cleared the table of their mess, depositing it into a waste can nearby. "Now, let's try to find the car!"

The four friends pulled up to Cheri and Tom's house and Charlotte was out of the car almost before it stopped. She seemed so anxious for them to meet her friends. "I just hope they can help. I know Tom's father was a Resistance fighter. I am not sure about Cheri's". They walked up to the house and Charlotte knocked on the door. A woman about Charlotte's age answered and embraced her. She greeted her and Marie Louise in French and then turned to Anne and John. "So pleased to meet with you," she said in barely recognizeable English. Anne thought her French was just about as good as Cheri's English. She smiled at the woman and held out her hand. "Comment allez vous?" she asked. At least she knew that much French! Cheri laughed and then greeted John, who greeted her in turn. She invited them in and bade them to sit in the parlor. They made small talk, such as it was, for a few minutes and then Charlotte came right to the point. "Cheri, didn't Tom's father help with that flier that went down? That American flier? We were hoping you could tell us a bit about it. John has reason to believe it might be his father in that unmarked grave." John started and said, "Well, Charlotte, I am not at all sure it is him. It's just another piece of the puzzle. I don't hold out a lot of hope." Charlotte looked at him steadily. "But you want something you can hold, something you can know, something of your father." She barely whispered the last line. "This is important to you, non?" "Well, yes, of course it is important." Charlotte looked at her friend and said something in French. Cheri looked a little startled and then nodded. "Un moment", she said and walked into the other room. She returned with a wooden box and put it gingerly on the coffee table. "These are some things of the flier's. We keep them in honor for him", Cheri said. She glanced at Charlotte and opened the box. She took out a button that looked like it came off an old uniform. Next she took out a man's comb that was warped. Lastly and with great care, she took out a wedding band and set it next to the other items on the table. Anne's hand shook as she picked it up to examine it more closely. She looked inside. She couldn't make out the inscription, just the words "Jack and Anne". But there was one other identifying mark that she recognized immediately. The double heart that Jack had scratched on it on their wedding night. "Two hearts joined are better than one," he had told her. This could not be anybody else's ring but her Jack's. That was her husband, John's father buried in an unmarked and hidden grave. Tears ran down her face. She grasped John's hand. "It's his, Jack's," she choked out the words and John put his arm around her. Charlotte and Marie Louise had tears in their eyes and Cheri hid her face in her hand. "Take it. His son should have it," she said. She glanced at Charlotte again and Charlotte agreed. "Yes, John, you must have a bit of your father." John reached out for the ring and took it. He still wore the ring that Cathy had given him years ago, so he put the ring on his right ring finger. His father had done physical work and his hands had been a little bit bigger than John's protected surgeon's hands. "Thank you," John said, standing and lifting his mother to her feet. "Now I know that my father is dead, approximately where he rests. It's been a long time coming for my mother, especially. And to have something of his. I never thought I would have anything. Thank you." Cheri seemed overcome by his gratitude and excused herself. Charlotte looked embarrased and Marie Louise looked bewildered. "Mama, what is wrong with Cheri? I had no idea she was so sensitive." Charlotte steered them all toward the front door. "One never knows how one will react when something like this happens. I don't suppose she ever thought she would find someone that knew the owner of those items even though she kept them all those years. Very emotional time for everyone." She took Anne's arm and helped her to the car. "Are you alright, Anne? You look so pale." She aided Anne into the front seat and then shut the door. Anne attempted a weak smile. "I'm alright. It is such a shock. I must say, I never expected to find much, least of all Jack's wedding band." And she burst into tears and could not seem to quit crying. Everyone tried to comfort her, but she urged them to start the drive back to Seaport Vue and she would collect herself presently, which is exactly what happened. As they pulled up in front of Madame Chevereaux' s, Charlotte patted Anne's shoulder. "Now you and Jean have what you need to rest your minds, non?" Anne reached from the front seat and covered the hand on her shoulder. "Yes, Charlotte, thank you for all your help and friendship." Charlotte said nothing and then withdrew her hand and exited the car. "Marie Louise and I will walk home," she called walking down the street.. "Marie Louise, supper tonight?" John asked. "Yes, at 7 pm?" "Oui, that's good. Pick you up or meet at the pub?" "Meet me at the pub!" John let go of her hand and smiled as she walked away. He seemed to suddenly remember his mother was still in the car and walked around to open the door for her. "Thank you, dear", she smiled up at him. She made a move to get out of the car, failed and sat back down on the seat. John lifted her out of the car and put an arm around her. "Mom, you are done in. I think we need to go home. I know you miss the family and we have been here 10 days. I don't want anything to happen to you." Anne leaned on him as he helped her into the Bed and Breakfast. "I am sorry Son. I don't mean to rain on your parade and I would like to see Paris. I mean, who comes to France and doesn't see Paris?" She tried to make a joke. John wasn't biting and walked her up the stairs to their rooms. "I want you to rest and I will make arrangements to fly back in a few days. Maybe we can stay in Paris a couple of days, maybe not. Let's see how you feel." He sat his mother down on her bed and took off her shoes. "Oh, John, to be saddled with me when you have a new romance budding. It's not fair," Anne told him. "Nonsense, I can come back and I haven't felt "saddled" with you at all. I am glad we came together. Neither of us has traveled much. I don't know why you and Dad didn't go to Japan when Jolene was there." Anne thought back to the time when the kids were gone all those years. Her heart had ached for them and yet, Luke did not want to visit them in Japan. There were some bad memories that just never went away and he had always had a hard time with forgiving Japan for bombing Pearl Harbor. He said he never wanted to see their country. Luke had rarely denied her much, but on this he was adamant. "Mom, you rest. I will have Madame Chevereaux make you a light supper. She will be happy for the extra money. Now, lie down and I am going to make arrangements for a plane ride home. Perhaps, if you feel a little better, we can spend a day and a night in Paris, we will see. I think I should get a Parisian doctor to look you over too," John said anxiously. Anne protested. "Oh, John, no, I am fine. I just get tired at my age, dear. With a little rest, I should be fine, but you are right, I do want to go home." She smiled up at him and he kissed her forehead. "Maybe that is why you and Dad never traveled. You both were homebodies." He helped her to lie down and covered her with a blanket. "Now, go to sleep. I will arrange for the flight. Sweet dreams." He turned off the light, closing the door to her room softly. Anne sighed. She didn't mind old age so much, except how it affected those around her. Maybe that's why she and Luke had always seemed so spry. They had the comfort of home and family and busied themselves in their small town making a difference. People used to stay closer to home, at least the people she knew. She really had no burning desire to travel, but she was glad she had come to France and had seen these beautiful little towns and met these fascinating people. And Jack, oh Jack, I finally know what happened to you. God rest your soul, my dearest love. I will see you again and it won't be long. She closed her eyes wearily and went right to sleep.

"So you will take your mama home now?" Marie Louise asked softly over a glass of her favorite red wine. John nodded. He hadn't realized how terribly hard it would actually be to leave her until the time had come. "I worry about her. She is much more frail over here than I ever noticed before. I don't want anything to happen to her. My family would never forgive me." He smiled lamely at her and she returned it. "You must look after dear Anne, she is so sweet. My mama likes her very much and so do I. We will talk and make plans later, non?" John nodded. "I booked a flight out for Tuesday morning, so it will give her a day to rest in Paris. I might want a doctor to look at her too, but she's adamant against that. She says I am a doctor and I can take care of her. Well, I am a general surgeon and that is a little different, but my prescription for her is rest and see her family again." They continued to hold hands across the table and then Marie Louise spoke. "I am glad you found what happened with your pere. It is important you and your mother know. It is, how you say, closure?" "Yes, that was what we came for and that is what we got. Time to go home. But, Marie Louise, I love you and I am not just going home and forget you. I will be in touch, alright?" She squeezed his hand gamely. "Of course alright. We will work something out. My heart has never felt like this and I rather like it!" She smiled that dimpled smile at him and he kissed her hand, clutched in his.

Charlotte stood at the car door, basket in hand. She had prepared a huge basket for them to take with them on the plane. John figured they could eat on it for a week! "Goodbye, dear Anne, I am so glad to have met you! No matter what, remember always that I think you are a very dear and kind person and I would never do anything to hurt you!" Anne looked at her. "What a strange thing to say, Charlotte. Of course you wouldn't!" Charlotte threw her arms around her. "Godspeed, dear friend. If things were different, we would be friends forever." "We will be friends forever, Charlotte. I won't say I will ever be over here again, but perhaps through the children, we will stay close, non?" Anne smiled as she used the French word at the end of the sentence that so many Frenchman used. "Oui, Anne," Charlotte said softly. John and Marie Louise were saying goodbye on the other side of the car. They had said their real goodbyes the night before and it was only because of their strong faiths that they had not stayed the night with each other. The wrenching was almost physical for John, almost as bad as when he lost Cathy for good. But he had a chance with Marie Louise, a chance at romantic love again and he was going to try with everything in him to make that happen. "I leave for my grandnephew's house today to help his wife with their new baby. She has three children already in four years and my nephew is hopeless. He has nobody left but his aunts and uncles and cousins and he is very special to me. So, my mind and body will be busy for the next week and it will help me with missing you." John hugged her to him. "I suppose my grandkids will help me with missing you, but I am going to work on something to get us together." She smiled up at him and kissed him. "And I know you will succeed!" The final goodbyes were over and they waved goodbye as they drove out of the town that had yielded so much for them.

Anne lounged on her bed in the luxurious hotel that John had booked, as he emailed the kids that they were returning home. John had booked the flight for the morning after next so they would have some time to sightsee if Anne felt up to it. If not, she could enjoy the luxury of the hotel and she did. "John, you are the kindest, most considerate son. This is a beautiful hotel and I am so relaxed. Why don't we go out for dinner tonight and then after a good night's rest, we could try some sightseeing? I know it's no fun alone." She smiled at him and he smiled back. "Well, Mom, if all goes according to plan, this won't be the last time I am in Paris. I know I am not a kid, but I feel like one right now." He looked so happy that it tugged at Anne's heart. Oh, how she hoped Marie Louise and John could work things out between them. "What time is it now?" John looked at his smartphone. "Wow, it's already 3:30 pm. Would you like to see some of the sights before dinner Mom? They eat late here." "I would love that," Anne replied and if to prove it, she bounced off her bed and went into the bathroom to prepare. What a sight Paris was! They could see the Eiffel Tower from their hotel room and it was hard for Anne to catch her breath. They decided to start with the Champ de Mars, where the Eiffel Tower was located. It was barely a 3 minute walk from their hotel and she felt vaguely like the first time she had seen Disneyland when she was in her 40's, overwhlemed. They strolled through the streets marveling at the many sights. There were pastry shops galore and fruit stands and flower stands. There was a small replica of the Statue of Liberty near the Seine and museums. They toured one museum until Anne pled fatigue and they sank down on a bench outside of it to catch their breaths. John glanced at his watch. "Wow, it is already 7:30 pm, can you believe that? What do you say we go to dinner and then get some of those French pastries to take up to our room? I haven't been able to get them off my mind since the first whiff!" His mother laughed and agreed and they reluctantly rose to their feet to find a restaurant. There were several to choose from and much outside seating and they finally found a small bistro that had a succulent sounding menu. John ordered for them, after telling Anne what was offered and the maitre d' left with a smile and a bow. The two relaxed at their table and watched the people interact on the busy street. "I love this," John said suddenly. "I like the differentness, the people, the whole idea. I am glad we came over here." Anne said nothing. She was glad they had closure about Jack and she was glad she met the people and saw the places she saw. But the good old US of A is where she belonged and where she always wanted to be and when they reached home, she would never leave it again. Besides once to Hawaii, she had never left the 48 states until now. She guessed she had just outlived her time. Everything was different and fast and frightening to her. But sitting here on the Champs de Mars in Paris, France with her 68 year old son, she did feel a sense of peace, like everything was now done and she could relax. She sighed contentedly. Their meal came and they ate in comfortable silence, soaking in the evening sights and sounds. They finished their wonderful coffee leisureably and then went in search of the fantastic pastries that John had seen. They finally found the right shop and bought 1/2 dozen that they would eat in their room for breakfast. They planned to sleep in.

Sleep in they did! It was 11:00 am before either one of them awakened, Anne first and she tiptoed into John's room to see if he was awake. He seemed to sense her presence, because he opened one eye and told her good morning. There was a coffee maker in the suite and Anne brewed some of the rich French coffee. Within 5 minutes, John had followed the aroma with his nose and was looking for the pastries that he remembered picking up last night. They talked and drank coffee and ate pastries and it was almost 12:30 pm before they were finished. Each wandered into their own room to get ready for a little sightseeing again and met again in the main suite about 1:30 pm. They went back to the

Champs de Mars to check out "Swan Lake" and look at the luxurious garden that bordered along the walks. Breathtaking, was all Anne could think to say. She knew there were so many other places they should be seeing, such as the Champs Elysees and the Arc de Triomphe, not to mention the Louvre, but she just couldn't tear herself away from this lovely place. John seemed content to just go at this slow place. They bought some more pastries and cheese, croissants, meat and fruit for dinner. They left out the wine, opting for fruit drinks that were popular with the locals. Anne thought they should get up to their rooms and pack, as they flew out of Charles de Gaulle Airport at 9:30am the next morning. The airport was about 15 miles away and John had already arranged for a 7:00 am shuttle. The hotel would graciously take care of getting their rental car back and they wouldn't have to bother with that at all. There were some perks to living like the rich and famous and Anne restrained herself, once again, from asking John if he was sure he could afford all this. They rode up the elevator clutching their treasured supper and entered their suite. While Anne put the food on the table, John started throwing his socks and underwear, the only thing he had unpacked, into the suitcase. "Come and eat, John. You can do that afterwards," his mother called. John rolled his eyes and then chuckled to himself. Some things never changed. They had a lively discussion about all the sights they had seen that day. They did ride the elevator up to the top of the Eiffel tower and back down again, getting off a one level to look at the view and then back down again. "I just wanted to say I was in the Eiffel Tower," Anne had told him. They had tried getting a table at the coveted restaurant of Alain Decasse, Le Jules Verne, but unfortunately it was booked well into six months. They weren't too disappointed because they hadn't really expected to get in, but it never hurt to ask. John drank his last drop of coffee and grabbed the last eclair grinning wickedly at his mother. "Sorry, mom, did you want this?" he asked, knowing she would acquiesce to him, however, she reached for the eclair and popped it into her mouth. John stood there with his mouth open and she laughed, a hearty open laugh, one he had not heard since before his father died and he had to laugh along with her. "Oh, John, you should have seen your face. Mommy took my eclair," she sputtered and she was laughing so hard that tears were running down her face. John was still laughing when she went to a napkin, unwrapped an eclair and handed it to him. "You are still my baby boy and I could never take the last eclair," she teased. He shook his head, stuck the eclair into his mouth before she could change her mind and went to finish his packing. He heard his mother humming in the other room. "I'll be glad when I don't have to worry about my passport all the time. It's kind of nerve wracking, you know?" she talked to him. "Uh-huh," he answered absent mindedly and then reached for his own passport. It was not there. He spoke silently to himself, telling himself to calm down, it was somewhere. As he searched for it to no avail, his calmness gave way to distress and then he finally asked his mother if she had seen it. "No, honey, the last place I saw it was in that little alcove at Madame Cheveneaux's, you know where you kept your wallet and phone and glasses when you went to bed." He stared at her for a minute and then hit his head. "And that is still where it is! I remember I picked up my wallet, phone and glasses and put them in my shirt and pants pockets and I thought I will get my passaport and put it in my suitcoat and then I got interrupted. I can't believe I did that! Mom, there is nothing to do but drive back to Seaport Vue tonight and get it. I have to have it. Thank God the hotel didn't take the car back yet. They told me earlier they would turn it in tomorrow morning. I'll be back in a couple of hours." Anne made a move to get her coat. "Don't be silly, I'll go with you. I know that Marie Louise isn't there, but I bought this sweet knickknack for Charlotte and instead of having the hotel mail it, I'll just give it to her." With that, she dug out the small replica of the Statue of Liberty that had "Amitie" written on it, which read in English as "Friendship". She stuck it into her purse and moved to the door. "Let's go," she said and he made sure he had his wallet, phone and glasses and his room key before he left. It took them about an hour and a half to make it to Seaport Vue and they got there about 8:30 pm. "I'll just drop you off at Charlotte's and I will run over to Madame Cheveneaux's and pick up my passport. We can only stay a minute, so get about a 5 minute visit in and I will be back shortly, okay?" "Sure, honey, I understand that we have a drive back. We are both too old not to need our beauty sleep," she said wryly and he smiled. "Can you get out okay by yourself?" he asked her. "I said I needed my beauty sleep not a wheelchair!" she retorted, pushing open the car door and stepping out. John chuckled, put the car in gear and drove toward the bed & breakfast in search of his passaport. Anne walked up to the now familiar house and knocked on the front door. Suddenly, she heard a familiar laugh. She froze. How could that be? John was at the bed & breakfast. Nobody had that laugh but him. Nobody alive anyhow. The door flew open and a laughing man with silver curly hair and a dimple in his chin stood there. She knew who it was, but she couldn't believe it. "Jack?" she whispered. "Non, Madame, I am Rene. And you are....?" He left the sentence unfinished and frowned at her. "Do I know you, Madame?" he asked, not realizing he was speaking English to her. Why would he know to speak English to her? "Jack, do you remember me, Anne?" His beautiful brown eyes became clouded and something akin to panic crossed his face. "Annie?" He looked at her uncomprehendingly. A woman's voice called out. "Who is it, darling?" and Charlotte appeared at his side. Her face blanched when she saw Anne. "Anne! I thought you were in Paris." Anne was speechless. The betrayal of Charlotte was almost too much to bear and the fact that Jack did not come home when he knew she was waiting was beyond comprehension. Jack just stood there, looking confused and Charlotte came out and took Anne's arm, moving her away from the door. "Anne, I can explain..." Anne turned on her, shaking her hand off her arm. "Really, Charlotte? You can explain? How can you explain that you let me and John make total fools of ourselves while all this time you knew that my husband was really your husband. Why didn't you just come out and tell me?" "Tell you? What would I tell you? That he does not know you, does not remember you? That I was afraid something might jar in his mind and I might lose him?" Anne scoffed. "Oh, please, Charlotte, after 60 years, that's ridiculous. You let me pour out my heart to you while you sat there laughing at me..." "Oh, Anne, non, non, never did I laugh. I cried much, my heart was so full for your pain. But it was 60 years ago and you had a husband and a good life and you had Rene's son." Anne cut her off. "How could you let my son and your daughter fall in love and know they were half brother and sister? It will break their hearts! I can't speak to you anymore, Charlotte, I just can't. You need to tell Marie Louise and I will try to find a way to tell John that they can never be together." She thrust the small gift she had bought for Charlotte into her hands. "Here, this is for you. I bought it for my friend, but that woman doesn't exist, so just throw it away." Anne started walking away as the tears started to rain down her face. "Anne, there is a letter that I asked Madame Cheveneaux to mail to you. It explains everything. Please, Anne, this is what is best for Rene." Anne didn't have the heart to answer. All she could think of was seeing Jack's face again, seeing the confusion and panic in his eyes. She couldn't do that to him, she couldn't. Charlotte said he didn't remember. Father had said his mind was like "Swiss cheese". No, Charlotte was to blame and only Charlotte. She saw headlights coming at her. John reached over to open the door, but she jerked it open before he had a chance and climbed into the car. "How come you're still not at Charlotte's?" he asked her. "She had company," she said. "Did you find your passport?" "Yes, ma'am, right where you said it would be. Oh, and Madame Cheveneaux said Charlotte brought down a letter and asked her to mail it to you, so she just gave it to me."

He handed her the letter and she put it in her purse. "I'll read it on the plane," she said.

Anne closed her eyes as the plane took off from the Charles deGaulle Airport. Check in had been painless, as it had been when they had flown in. Both she and John had souveniers for everyone in the family in their stowed luggage and some of the wonderful Parisian pastries in a carryon bag. Anne sighed as she re-lived the night before. Seeing Jack again had been a shock, a terrible and wonderful shock. She wanted to go back and hug him and hold him and tell him how much she had missed him and show him his son, his first child, John. She wanted to tell him what he had missed and talk about his life, no she really didn't want to talk about his life. What had happened? Charlotte said she explained it all in the letter. Charlotte! She could hardly think of her without hate. This woman who had treated her so kindly and with so much love, this woman who she thought might one day be John's mother-in-law, she hated, hated! She had cheated her out of a husband she had loved with all her heart and John out of a wonderful father. No, she could never forgive, no matter what the Bible said. She was nearing the end of her life and she supposed now she wouldn't go to heaven because she wouldn't forgive, but she wanted to hang onto that hate. She had never hated anyone, not even the person that had shot down Jack's plane. She had even prayed for that person, but not Charlotte. She had knowingly and with aforethought malice (she hadn't been married to a lawyer for 60 years for nothing) connived to deceive her and John, the woman they came to for help. She glanced over at John who was fast asleep. Well, he was no spring chicken, either, she thought. I can't believe I am the mother of an old man. She opened her purse and dug out the envelope with her address on it, with USA written at the bottom, the letter from Charlotte. Opening the envelope, she read:

My dearest Anne:

There is a priest a few towns away who writes good English and it is to him that I made my confession and who writes this letter with his hand as I dictate it. You will no doubt be angry when you hear what I have to say, but please, read the entire letter before you judge me.

Let me start by saying I did not want to like you the way I did. You are a wonderful lady, Anne, so kind and sweet. I know why Rene married you. Yes, Rene, my husband Rene, is your Jack. I am sorry I had to deceive you, but it is not like you think. Rene does not remember anything before he crashed. His plane crashed near the beach here and my father and several men from the village ran down to put out the fire before the Nazis could see it. Rene had been thrown clear and was unconscious, but seemed okay otherwise. The men put him on a large piece of wood and carried him to our house. We were kind of the unofficial hospital and Dr. Colbert came quickly, as usual. He dressed some third degree burns on his hands and then he realized that he had many broken bones, plus a severe head injury. It was touch and go for a long time and I helped Mama and Papa take care of him. I became very fond of him, even though he had not regained consciousness. We could not find any dogtags. We had helped other Americans and they had all had dogtags so we could find their unit, but not this man. When he finally regained consciousness, he did not know anything about himself even his name, so they gave him the name, Rene, which means reborn. He was very frightened, almost panicked because of this and we tried to calm him down by giving him a past. We pretty much gave him Father Jacques' real past. That is why their lives sounded almost parallel. He spoke fluent French and English and he wanted to know why,

95

so we told him the priest had taught him. Father Pierre had been killed already, so it didn't matter, that little lie. He wept for the man he thought had raised him. Anne, you told me Jack had been raised in an orphanage, so I guess I didn't really lie to him. Slowly, we became better acquainted and our friendship grew, however, I was only 15 and Rene looked to be probably 20 or so. (I found out later from you that he was 22, so I guess my father was right to make us wait a year). Everything was so uncertain at that time and we were all marrying younger. Meanwhile (Father) Jacques had been captured as a Resistance fighter and the men made plans to rescue him. They knew that all or some of them might not survive. Rene wanted to go also and even though he was still weak, they let him. As it turned out, he was quite heroic, diverting the Nazi interrogaters by different noises he could make. Did you know he could throw his voice? He had them all out looking while the other men freed Jacques and carried him out. They thought they had lost him to the Nazis, but he rejoined them halfway home. I do not know the details and Rene never told me. We nursed (Father)Jacques at our home too and since Rene was living here, they became close friends. Finally, after VE day, Rene and I were married and had a typical small town post war wedding, no frills and not much food, but we were happy.

Yes, Anne, some men came after the war. Rene did not understand what they wanted with him and would not meet with them, so they never saw him. Perhaps they would have recognized him if they did, but Anne, I did not tell him not to see them. He begged me not to reveal him and so we did not. Only a few in town knew he was not French, just the men who had rescued him and the doctor and they all agreed not to betray him. I know, Anne, you think you were betrayed and maybe you were, but you did not see him at that time. If I thought he had a wife, (I did not discover the wedding ring until after my parents had died and I was cleaning out some drawers and found the box with those keepsakes) perhaps I would have had him talk to the men, but I don't think so. I was 16 years old and I loved my husband. Our country was war torn and we were all clinging to each other. I cannot ask you to understand why I did what I did, nor why I continued to deceive you, I can only ask that you forgive me and know I have loved your Jack all these years but in reality, Anne, he stopped being your Jack when that plane crashed. He never did regain his memory, ever. As you can see, he had six children after Jean and several grandchildren, so he has led a full life.

You are a wonderful person, one that I hated to lie to because you are so truthful and kind. I gave Cheri the button and comb and ring to give to you, but I really did think that Jean should have his father's wedding band. I am glad for that even if I had to deceive him with it. As for the children, Anne that is an awful consequence. Perhaps they liked each other so much because of family traits. They both are obviously hard to please when it comes to a mate and maybe liked the traits they saw in each other because they were the same ones they possessed themselves. Well, dear Anne, this is my story and I knew I must tell you for the childrens' sakes. They can never be married or even be together. I will do my best to soften the blow to Marie Louise. I never in my wildest dreams ever thought I would have to tell her this. Dear Anne, please try to find it in your heart to forgive me. I remain now and always,

Affectionately,
Charlotte

Anne laid the letter aside and wept. She wept for the love she and Jack never got to share. She wept for their unborn children. She wept for John missing out on having Jack as a father. She wept for Charlotte as a 16 year old bride trying to protect her husband and for Jack as a frightened young amnesiac, clinging to the only people he knew. She bowed her head, thanking God for how it had all turned out, not how she had envisioned it, but good nonetheless. John did have a father and she did have a loving husband. Jack had a houseful of children and Charlotte had kept her horrors at bay by having Jack to love. She asked forgiveness and asked Him to forgive Charlotte through her, because she just couldn't do it by herself. She felt somewhat better and felt the sweet peace come over her. She turned towards her sleeping son and touched his shoulder.